Change of Plans

BY

LaTosha Franklin

ISBN 978-1-943159-07-9

The publisher would appreciate notification where errors occur so that they may be corrected in subsequent printing and/or editions. Please send comments to the publisher by emailing to deeprivers67@yahoo.com

Printed in the United States of America

If you want to make God laugh…

Uptight Instruction Writer, Danius Todd has his entire life planned down to the minute. That is until he meets rocker-chick, Pearl McClure and her band-mates. Now his neat and tidy world has turned upside down. After chasing down his little brother, who stowed away in the band's tour van, and having his mother's car stolen, Danius must now depend on Pearl and her friends to get him and his brother home. But if he wants to get home he has to accompany the band on their tour, where he gets way more than he bargained for, he gets an adventure.

When he loses his heart and all his best laid plans are nowhere to be found, will Danius reach out to the One who has always held his destiny in the palm of His hand?

Change of Plans
By
LaTosha Franklin

An American author by the name of Annie Dillard once said, "A schedule defends from chaos and whim…" Though this author wasn't known to Danius Anthony Todd, he seemed to live by this saying. He held his schedule like a sword against anything that was spur-of-the-moment, off-the-cuff- or willy-nilly. He held *on* to his daily routine like a woman holds on to a 50% off designer blouse. He hated uncertainty. It was so…uncertain. He liked knowing where he was going and what he was doing and what time he was doing it.

On this day he knew exactly what he was going to do.

Wake up – 6am.
Shower and dress – 6:30am.
Breakfast – 6:45am
On the bus – 7am
This is Danius's morning routine. Now on any other day he would follow this by:

Arriving at work – 8am
Have lunch – 12pm
Return to work – 1pm
Leave work – 5pm
Dinner with family – 6pm
Refuse Dad's offer for a ride home, weather permitting, -
8pm
Arrive home – 9pm
Call girlfriend, Alexandria – 9:30pm
Watch ten o'clock news – 10pm
Bed – 10:30pm
Repeat

The slightest change would require a reworking of his entire schedule, which was what he was doing the day he met…

Pearl Marietta McClure cut up a banana and added the slices to her bowl of Cheerios then drizzled honey all over it. Now one might ask, "Why not just buy Honey Nut Cheerios?" But Pearl concluded that while Honey Nut Cheerios taste good, boredom quickly sets in when every O tastes like honey. At least this way you get a surprise with every spoonful. You may get honey, you may not. You may get banana, you may not. Sometimes you get both banana and honey. It keeps breakfast interesting. Pearl also took this approach to life: keep it interesting.

After breakfast Pearl grabbed her daily devotional bible. She called her devotion time *mini-church* and the word for the day came from Proverbs 16:9, *The human mind plans the way but the Lord directs the steps.*

"Okay, Lord." Pearl said. "I don't know what today has in store, but I thank you for directing my steps." With that she was off.

As she left her apartment complex in her Volks-Wagon Beetle, she came up alongside her elderly neighbor. "Hey, Miss Linda. Where are you off to?" she asked.

"Oh, good morning, Pearl. I'm just on my way to the salon."

"Well, save your bus fare. I'll drop you off."

"Thank you, but I don't want to take you out of your way."

"It's no problem. Besides you want to get there before ol' what's-her-name does and starts flirting with the barber, don't you?"

"I'm sure I don't know what you're talking about."

"Uh huh. You ain't foolin' nobody, Miss Linda. Get in."

Miss Linda laughed heartily as she situated herself in Pearl's compact car.

"I saw him checking you out last time." Pearl joked.

"You saw no such thing. And even if you did it doesn't matter as long as Ester Gray has her claws sunk in him."

"Wow. It's kind of like high-school with old people."

"I beg your pardon. Who are you calling *old*, young lady? Ester's the one with a foot in the grave."
Pearl beat the steering wheel as she laughed. "If that's the case then you might have a chance."

"Ain't that the truth?"

They laughed together as Pearl maneuvered the car around a city bus and joined the morning traffic.

"Ugh! Traffic." Danius muttered as he looked out the city bus window. One of the things he didn't like about public transportation was being at the mercy of the bus driver's schedule, mainly because it didn't coincide with *his* schedule. Why did the bus driver always have to take a ten minute break at this time? Didn't he realize if he kept going he could avoid the morning rush?

"I'll be glad when I get this laser surgery done on my eyes so I can get my license back and drive myself to work." said Danius's seat-mate and the other thing he didn't like about public transportation.

"But then again, if I was driving myself, I'd still be stuck in this traffic."
Danius gave the man a tight smile and a nod then checked the calendar on his i
Phone.

"My wife keeps telling me I should let my son drive me to work." The man said. "But that's like pulling teeth and I wouldn't want to ride in that death trap of his anyway. For one thing, his gas pedal broke off and all he has left is the stem. And he's riding around town just as happy as you please. He's in construction and landscaping so instead of seats, the back is full of his tools. There's no place to sit except on the floor. And it's not like he doesn't have the money to buy a new van or at least fix the one he has. The boy makes good money. He's just cheap. How I ever raised such a cheap son, I'll never know. But I tell you that boy is tight with a dollar."

With another smile and nod, Danius thought to himself, "*Just one more year*." If he could endure public transportation for one more year, he'd have enough money to pay cash for a nice pre-owned car and he could scratch that goal off his list.

***

"Here's the list of songs we're going to do for our tour." said Cary the second lead vocalist in the band for which Pearl sang and played keyboard.

"Cool. You guys want to go over these from the top?" Pearl asked the band.

"Sure." said Cary. "But let's go over the new one you wrote, too. I was thinking we could add it somewhere in the middle of the set."

"What? After weeks of hashing and rehashing our current set list, you want to add another song? We've only practiced it once."

"I know, but last night I had an epiphany."

"That sounds painful." said Michael the drummer.

"I'm sure there's a topical cream for that." said Emily the bass player.

Cary grabbed his side and sarcastically said, "Oh my gosh! Oh my gosh! You guys are hilarious. Can we rehearse, please? And you, Pearl, don't go pretending to be all shy with your song. You know it's good and I know we've only practiced it once, but that's what sheet music is for, right?"

"Sir, yes sir." said Pearl. "All right, let's do it."

"All right! Oh, before I forget, check out my new digital wireless guitar system. Ain't it sweet?"

Pearl bent down to inspect the new wireless amplifier. "That is nice. How does it work?"

***

Just follow the instructions. That's all anyone has to do. Danius found it a huge waste of time to field complaint calls. It was usually the same thing: some guy assembles an entertainment system all wrong and now his wife is calling in to complain about it crashing to the floor. His answer is always the same though. Just follow the instructions. That's not so difficult, unless the instructions are in Japanese and you don't happen to speak Japanese. But Danius didn't write instructions in Japanese, so what was the problem?

"My TV, my stereo system, all my kids' pictures and my grandmother's urn all fell to the floor. I had to vacuum half of my grandmother's ashes up. Parts of my grandmother are gone forever. How am I going to explain that at the family reunion? Now my husband insists that there was something wrong with the instructions. He followed them to a tee, but he had all these pieces left over."

"Well, ma'am I do apologize for the inconvenience and your grandmother's...remains." said Danius. "However, I'm sure if your husband followed the instructions carefully but still had parts left over, then this may be a manufacturing problem. Why don't you give them a call? Here's the number."

Danius gave the angry customer the number and removed his head-set.

"What was that all about?" asked his supervisor.

"A guy built an entertainment system, didn't follow instructions, now his grandmother's ashes are all over the place." he answered.

"Mmm. Been there. Oh well, what can we do? We're instruction writers not miracle workers. Anyway I know you don't need it, but I came to remind you about your meeting with Frederick Maxwell. He wants you to write the instructions for his new computer program. It's at 2pm so don't be late. But of course you won't be because you're...you."

"Yes sir. I won't forget. I'll be there." Danius declared proudly. He didn't have a late bone in his body. Even puberty arrived on schedule. He prided himself on punctuality and had no patience for procrastinators, but this meeting would interrupt his routine. It was being held at a café nearby. That meant leaving the office and Danius never left the office before 5pm.

Nevertheless, by 2pm Danius was seated at a table inside *The Q Café*, a café that boasted Q for Quality. He was sitting there readjusting his schedule, just minding his own business when…

Danius, meet Pearl

"Excuse me."

Danius looked up to find the brightest smile he'd ever seen directed right at him. The owner of that smile was a jean-clad, flip-flop wearing girl with a t-shirt depicting Michael Jackson in his legendary pose on his toes. She had skin the color of dark- chocolate with eyes to match. She had a mop of black dreadlocks with reddish brown high-lights. Odd, but Danius could swear she was radiating light from within. She rested her palms on the table and leaned forward.

"I'm sorry to interrupt, but my friends and I are trying to rehearse and we were wondering if you could keep it down."

Danius, dumbfounded, could barely string two words together. "Uh…I didn't…I mean I wasn't…I was just sitting…"

"Oh it's all right. Don't apologize." She sat down across from him as if they were old friends. "I guess you don't care for our kind of music."

"I don't…I mean I've never heard you. It's my first time here."

"I know."

"You know?"

"Yes. You know how I know? I've never seen you before. What's your name?"

She spoke kind of fast. When Danius's brain caught up to the conversation he answered. "Danius."

"Wow!" she said, looking genuinely amazed. "That's an interesting name. You know, I have a thing for interesting names. Does it mean anything?"

"No. Just that my mother wanted to name me Daniel and my father wanted to name me Dennis. They compromised."

She laughed. "I like your parents already. My name is Pearl. Now I know what you're thinking. What's a young, modern, woman such as myself doing with an old-school name like Pearl? Well my mother had a thing for jewelry, you know, gems and precious stones and what-not. She named my brother Jasper and my sister Ruby, but I got stuck with Pearl. It's okay though. I've learned to love it. Let me guess, you're waiting for somebody, right?"

Finally, he thought. *A way out of this conversation.* "Yes I am." Danius said. "He should be here any minute. So if you don't..."

"Oh I don't mind. I just thought I'd keep you company. You looked a little out of your element. I know what that's like. You know I was kidding about your keeping it down. I just wanted to come over to see what you looked like. I've been watching you for the past half-hour and the whole time your face was glued to your phone."

"Well I have a strict schedule that I have to keep."

"Schedules are important. That's for sure. You should've seen the type of schedule I used to keep not five years ago. I'm talking about me in a feminine version of a power suit, high-heels clack-clack-clacking back and forth down the hallway rushing from one meeting to the next in the busiest city in the world, New York. I mean I'd catch a cab to go to one meeting and a train to go to the next. I'd go home only to have my boss call me at three in the morning to tell me to catch a plane somewhere. *'I need you to go to Denver to meet with so and so on Monday. I need you to go to L.A. and have so and so sign the contract on Tuesday and take your passport because I need you to meet me in Canada on Wednesday for a meeting.'*

'I'm telling you it was killing me. I finally had to quit for my own health. If I hadn't scheduled bathroom breaks I'd probably be on a waiting list for a kidney right now. Of course I'm not opposed to schedules, you understand. But when you're living off of bagels, M&Ms and energy drinks, something's got to give. I mean, your schedule should never be so strict as to not have time to eat a well-balanced meal, right? Anyway, I hope *your* schedule is lenient enough to allow you time to listen to us play. We're going to rehearse a new song in a minute. I'm gonna come back over here and ask your opinion. Now I want you to be honest. Don't sugar-coat it just because you like me."

"Like you?"

"You do, don't you? Remember, your honest opinion." She walked away leaving a very bewildered Danius behind.

Momentarily stunned, he couldn't do anything but listen. Pearl sat at a keyboard and began to play a nice melody. Then her voice filled the café. A sweet, clear sound enveloped Danius and he found himself hanging on to every word.

I think I'm going to love you
Think I'll be thinking of you
In the middle of the night with the moonlight
Shining in my window
I know you don't know my name
But I hope you feel the same
Do you care that I cry and stay up all night
Thinking 'bout tomorrow?
Then you look at me
And I'm at a loss for words

A love song? Somehow Danius couldn't equate this girl with a soft ballad. For the second verse, the key went up and Pearl looked directly at him and sang:

Did you just look at me?
Or am I seeing things
Did you smile at me and wave your hand?
Or am I just dreaming?
Oh yes I do believe
It's the beginning
Of the rest of our lives with you by my side
Or is it wishful thinking?
But then you look again. And I'm at a loss for
words

Suddenly the rest of the band joined in and the rock sound that Danius expected began to rise out of this ballad, as did Pearl. She got up from the keyboard, grabbed an electric guitar and stood at a microphone. Another guitarist, a man, stood to her left and sang:

For the first time in a long while
I feel like a child
Shy and afraid to smile

Then Pearl added a bit of edge to her voice and sang:

And for the first time in a long time
Now that you look my way
I don't know what to say
I'm at a loss...

The music stopped as the drummer counted one, two, three, four. Then it picked back up with the male guitarist playing rhythm, another female guitarist playing bass and Pearl playing the melody on lead guitar. They played the chorus and then ended together.

Danius was no judge of music, but they sounded just as good, if not better, than any professional band he'd ever heard. If he could fit a concert into his schedule, he'd pay money to hear them. The handful of people in the café clapped as Pearl made her way off stage and back to Danius's table.

"Well what'd you think? Give it to me straight." she said. There was that light again. Danius actually felt warmed by it.

"It was very good." he said nervously. "I don't know much about music, but you were all very good."

"I agree." said the man sitting next to Danius at the table. For the second time in ten minutes, Danius was dumb-founded. It was Mr. Maxwell.

iPhone lost, iPhone found

"Mr. Maxwell?" Danius hadn't even noticed him sitting there. "I'm sorry…I didn't… I was listening to…I didn't see you…"

"That's quite all right, Todd. You were enjoying the music." Mr. Maxwell said, and then looked at Pearl. "So was I. That was very good, young lady."

"Thank you, sir. I'm glad you liked it. We're adding that song to our set when we go on tour day after tomorrow."

"It's so good to hear young people playing real instruments. I'm afraid Guitar Hero is the closest my son will ever get to it."

"Oh!" Pearl laughed. "Don't be discouraged. He's probably good at a lot of things."

"He does have a good head for business…for a ten-year-old."

"So did my brother when he was that age. He was always washing cars, cutting grass, painting houses. The other kids made fun of him, but now he's twenty-four and runs his own restaurant supply business today?"

"Really? That's amazing." said Mr. Maxwell.

"Straight out of high-school, I'm telling you."

Within minutes of meeting Pearl, she'd already teased Danius about keeping a schedule, distracted him so that he didn't even know Mr. Maxwell was sitting right next to him and now she was monopolizing all of Mr. Maxwell's time. It was time to take back control. "Yes and speaking of business," he said. "Mr. Maxwell and I should be getting down to it."

"About that, Todd," Mr. Maxwell said. "This new program is very intricate. It'll take more than a lunch meeting to learn it. I was thinking, why don't you join my family and me Friday night at our beach house on the coast? Stay the weekend. It'll take that long to go through the entire program."

"Oh, well. Mr. Maxwell…I don't know. On Fridays my girlfriend and-"

"Oh, bring her along. We have plenty of room." Mr. Maxwell said, looking at Pearl. "I think you're charming. I know my wife would think so too. You know, she's a musician herself."

"Really?" Pearl asked.

"Yes. Classical."

"I was trained in classical piano, I never appreciated it as a kid, but now I really love it."

"Maybe the two of you can get together…"

"No!" Danius exclaimed. "She can't come… she's…she's not my…I don't know…"

"Well, what Danius is trying to say is that the band is going on tour and we'll be in West Palm Beach on Friday." Pearl clarified. "Otherwise I would love to go Mr. Maxwell."

"Call me Frederick."

"Frederick: Peaceful ruler." Pearl looked as if the name Frederick was the cutest, most precious thing on Earth.

"That's right." Mr. Maxwell – Frederick – said, flattered that someone else knew what his name meant. "You know, the beach house is only a couple…six hours' drive from West Palm. If you and the band can make it, I do wish you'd come. You see, Saturday is my wife's birthday, it's going to be a very formal affair and I'd like to have live music. Now I noticed you have a jazzy, kind of rock sound. Do you know any jazz standards?

"Oh sure we do, thanks to Patrick, our lead guitarist and manager. He's a connoisseur of all things jazz. I tell you what, Frederick I'll talk it over with the others and see what they think."

"Please do. And of course I'll make it worth your while. Tell the band to name a fair price."

"I sure will!" Pearl looked over at Danius and said, "What do you think about that; you and I working for the same man? It's providence I tell you."

Mr. Maxwell laughed heartily.

"It's…something else." Danius answered through clinched teeth.

"S'wonderful, S'marvelous…" Pearl sang.

This made Mr. Maxwell laugh in earnest and say, "Oh, Todd, now I'm convinced. You have to persuade your charming girlfriend to join us. What was your name again?" He asked Pearl.

"Well it *was* Michelle Obama, but for obvious reasons I changed it to Pearl McClure."

They laughed like old friends, all except Danius.

"Todd, where ever did you find such an enchanting girl?"

"I didn't find her. She found me and she's not my girlfriend."

"That's true Frederick." said Pearl. "Danius and I are just friends, but we go way back. How long has it been, Danius, 13, 14…minutes?"

Pearl smiled.

Mr. Maxwell laughed.

Danius stewed.

Mr. Maxwell stood to leave. "Nevertheless, I want you all to come. Here's my card." He handed a card to the both of them. "Miss Pearl, I do hope to see you this weekend. And Todd, I can count on you to be there, right?"

"Well…uh…I…yes sir."

"Good. You'll have to excuse me. I have another meeting across town. Todd, I'll call you later this evening with further details." Mr. Maxwell gave Danius a heavy-handed slap on the back.

"Yes sir." A defeated Danius said.

"It was a pleasure meeting you, Pearl" Mr. Maxwell warmly shook Pearl's hand. Pearl smiled. She really was pretty and probably enchanting, Danius thought, but at the moment, *annoying* was the only adjective he'd use to describe her.

Mr. Maxwell left and Pearl called out to her band mates and said, "Hey guys, we just got offered a paying gig this Saturday night on the coast. What do you think?

As one they all shouted, "Awesome!" and started another jam session. Danius felt as if he were trapped inside of a musical.

Pearl looked at him and smiled. "Looks like we'll see you there. Hey, genius idea! You wanna carpool? We got plenty of room in the van. You don't get car sick riding sideways, do you?"

"No. And no thank you to the ride. Look Ms. McClure…"

"We're friends now. Call me Pearl."

"Okay Pearl. I don't know what just happened here, but now I have to readjust my schedule and I can't help but think that this is all your fault."

"My fault? Did *I* invite you to *my* beach house on the coast? And what are you complaining about? You get to spend two days and two nights on the sandy shores of the Florida coast, breathing sea air and waking up to a beautiful view of the ocean. If you stay up late enough, you might even spot sea turtles on the shore. But something tells me you adhere to a strict bedtime."

"Well I have to wake up early. And that's not the point."

"What is the point?"

"The point is I was supposed to meet Mr. Maxwell here for lunch, discuss his new program, go back to work and get started on writing the instructions for it. That was the plan. Now all of a sudden I'm expected at his wife's birthday party to which you, a complete stranger, are now invited and to spend the weekend at their house. I can't go to the coast for a weekend. My girlfriend and I had plans. We always have lunch at The Bistro. Then we visit the museum or take in a matinee. On Sundays we go to church and then have brunch with her parents."

"Where you go through the Sunday paper together?" Pearl asked.

Danius chose not to answer that question. "Listen." he said. "What I mean is that I have my days scheduled in such a way that I always know where I'm going and what I'm doing. I live a very-

"Structured life." Pearl said.

"Right. And I rarely ever-

"Deviate from the plan."

"If I can help it. Besides, Alexandria is a serious-minded person and-

"She wouldn't approve of going to a party."

"No. And will you please-

"Stop finishing your sentences? Yes I will."

Danius "harrumphed" like a grumpy, old man and then began to gather his belongings. Enchanting or not, this girl definitely had a screw loose. He might have laughed at that thought if he wasn't so annoyed.

Pearl took pity on him. "Oh, Danius don't be upset. Life has a funny way of throwing a stick into your bicycle spokes. First you're riding along, minding your own business and then, *bam!*" Her "bam" startled Danius, making him drop all of his things on the floor. "See?" Pearl said bending to help him. "Next thing you know, you've just fallen head over heels..." Their hands brushed against each other and their eyes met. "...and there's nothing you can do about it." she whispered.

The brief contact sent a tingling sensation from his fingers to his brain then to every nerve ending and Danius entertained the thought of kissing a complete stranger. But he quickly shook that idea off. "I have to go." he said and finished gathering up his things and walked out without so much as a backwards glance.

Pearl stared at his retreating back and then the door after he was gone. *What a sweet guy.* She thought. *Wound a little tight, but sweet.* And handsome! He had caramel colored skin and jet black hair that was cut close to his head and his eyes were nearly as dark. Oh he was a beautiful man, but he had the look of a little lost boy; sort of unsure of himself. Pearl smiled.

This was new. She found lots of men attractive looking, but could never say she was attracted to them. But when Danius looked up from his iPhone, she felt that undeniable "spark" that she'd heard tell of. "Whoa." She said and shook her head. Her hand still tingled where his fingers brushed across it. When she happened to look down, she spotted his iPhone underneath the table. He was long gone by now, she thought, but that was all right. Now she knew she would see him again.

A stick in the bicycle spokes

"Where is it? Where is it?" Danius muttered to himself. He had turned his briefcase and his apartment upside down looking for his phone and couldn't find it. He felt a moment of panic because all of his important information was in that thing. "What did I do with it?" Then her face flashed in his mind. "Oh, no." He sighed. He left his iPhone at the café which meant he'd have to go back, which meant he'd have to see "her" again; Miss Stick-In-My-Bicycle-Spokes."

In nearly one hour a complete stranger had turned Danius's whole day upside down and just when he thought he'd be free of her, it turned out he had to see her again. "What else can happen?"

The telephone let out its annoying shrill and when Danius answered it the unmistakable southern twang of his mother's voice answered back. "Hi, honey. Did I catch ya' at a bad time?"

Yes. Today is Wednesday not Thursday. I always talk to you on Thursdays. "Uh…no, Mom. I was just looking for my iPhone. Is everything all right?

"Everything's wonderful! Your father surprised me with cruise tickets. Eeeeee! She screamed in delight. Danius held the phone away from his ear until she was finished. "We leave for the Bahamas on Friday." she said.

"That's great Mom."

"I know. I'm so excited. There's so much I have to do. First, I was wondering if you could watch your brother while we're gone."

"What? Mom I can't. I…I have a business meeting this weekend and Alexandria…well you know how she is around Josiah."

"I made him apologize for throwin' up on her. Honestly, when is she gon' let that go?"

"It's not just that. I mean what am I supposed to do with him?"

"Danius, he's your brother. Hang out with him. Take him to the park or that video game place he likes. There's not a whole lot you have to do with a twelve-year old except make sure he stays out of trouble and doesn't get any body parts caught in anything. Besides it's only for a week. We'll give you some money and you have my permission to buy him all the junk food he's not allowed to eat at home. I know I'm springing this on you all of a sudden but you'd be doing us a huge favor. Please honey?"

"But I'd have to rearrange my entire schedule."

"Oh, Danius, won't you please do this for your mama? It would mean so much to me. I don't wanna be in the middle of the Atlantic worried about my baby. I wanna have fun."

His mother wasn't the "guilt-trip" type, but he did indeed feel guilty. After all, the woman lives for her men: Her husband, Gary and her sons, Danius and Josiah; how she had sacrificed for him most of his life and even now. And when Danius was determined to live on his own, it was she who kept him from starving or poisoning himself with his own cooking. Watching his little brother was the least he could do.

"Okay, Mom."

"Oh thank you, thank you, thank you!"

Stick Number 2

"What!" Alexandria yelled into the phone.

"Now, Alexandria it's just for a week." Danius tried to explain. "My parents are going on a cruise and…"

"And there was no one else your brother could stay with?"

"Yes…no…I mean you're right. There's no one else he could stay with."

"Well, what about our plans for the weekend?"

"We can still do what we planned. We just have to take Josiah with us."

"I just don't know how that's going to be possible."

"Well, why not?" Danius asked.

"Danius, I don't see much wisdom in spending the weekend with a child who causes me to break out in rashes." Alexandria said.

"That was only once and only because he was wearing a wool sweater when he hugged you. Besides you didn't break out the last time you saw him."""

"That's because I was too busy cleaning vomit off of my suede boots."

"Well, that proves it then. You're allergic to wool not the boy." Danius heard Alexandria's long drawn-out sigh over the phone.

"I'm sorry, Danius, but we're just going to have to cancel our plans this weekend."

"But Alexandria…"

"It's nothing against your brother. It's strictly for my health. You understand."

Danius sighed. "Yes. I guess so."

Stick Number 3

"Sweetheart, I forgot to tell you, your brother's taken a vow of silence, but he won't tell us why. So you may have some difficulty communicatin'."

"Difficulty?! Mom!" Danius exclaimed over the phone.

"Oh, don't worry, Sweetheart. He's not suicidal. He's just gettin' in touch with his artistic side. You know, he always did have an admiration for mimes. Yesterday he did the walking down the stairs thing. It was so cute."

"What am I supposed to do with a mute kid, Mother?"

"You'll just have to be creative. It's not hard. You just communicate with him on his level."

"I can't believe you're actually allowing him to do this."

"It's important to support a child's natural talents and creativity. It's like when you were his age and you insisted on doing our taxes. We didn't stop you, did we? We had a pretty nice return too."

After the conversation ended, Danius sat down on his modest, little sofa and tried to make sense out of his day. *I met a strange girl. I've been invited to a birthday party. I lost my iPhone. My plans for the weekend have been canceled. I'm spending the week with my brother who refuses to speak. And she was right about the sticks in my bicycle spokes.*

How did that crazy girl from the café pop back into his mind? She had no business being there in the first place, and now here she was for the second time since he'd met her three hours ago. There was something about that girl that made Danius shake his head. What sort of person quits a prestigious corporate job to loaf around with a bunch of slacker musicians?

"Obviously someone who can't hack it in the real world." He said out loud to no one.

No doubt about it. She was a flake and Danius had no patience for flaky people. The sooner he got his phone back, the sooner Pearl McClure would be out of his life and out of his head.

Slowly Unraveling

The next day, the café hadn't opened yet when he phoned before work, so Danius had to hang in there until lunch. It wasn't easy, he felt lost without his phone and planner; like a ship without a rudder or a kite without a string. When lunch time finally rolled around, he hurried like an anxious little squirrel towards the café only to find out his iPhone wasn't there and neither was Pearl.

"But she left this note for you in case you showed up." said the cashier to a frustrated Danius.

Danius opened the note and read: *Dear Danius- hope I spelled it right.*

If you're reading this note that means I haven't returned from South Carolina.

"South Carolina! What is she doing in South Carolina?"

The cashier shrugged his shoulders and pointed to the note. Danius continued reading.

I had to come to S.C. to visit my great-grandmother. She's competing in the X-games and I wanted to support her...just kidding. But seriously, it was her 93rd birthday and you know how it is with old people. Every birthday is an achievement. Don't worry though. I have your phone and I'm guarding it with my life. I should be back by tonight. Meet me at the café at seven.

Danius began to feel a dull ache behind his eyes. With his chin to his chest and slumped shoulders, he made his way back to work, resigning himself and his iPhone to the mercy of a weird stranger.

For the first time in years Danius's well controlled life was unraveling. Without his phone it seemed to Danius that things were happening without his expressed, written consent. His life was in that thing including the time, which is why he never wore a watch. Now he found himself having to ask for help; with appointments, contact lists, remembering notes, the correct time for goodness sake. He even did something he hadn't done in a while: asked God to help him remember an important detail from a past meeting. And then a thought occurred to him. Exactly when did he *stop* asking for God's help? It troubled him briefly but he didn't have time to examine why, because just as he was leaving the office, his parents pulled up with Josiah, the man of mystery.

"Hi, honey." Gloria Todd said. She was the first to get out and greet Danius.

"Hi, Mom. Dad. Josiah. What are you all doing here?"

"I know it's earlier than we planned, but we were talking and we decided it would be better to drive down to Miami tonight and stay in a hotel, then board the ship in the morning."

"It's a six hour trip from here to Miami." Dad said. "Seven with your mom's pottie breaks."

"Now, Gary, you know that's not true." Mom said. "But we did want to get on the road and beat the traffic. Is it all right that we bring Josiah here?"

Again with the spur of the moment decisions. "Well, I'm on my way to the café' where I left my phone." Danius said. "But I guess he can come with me."

"Oh good. And thanks again, honey. You're a life saver."

Then Gary Todd walked around to the curb and deposited seven, crisp twenty-dollar bills into Danius's hand. "He likes those pizza rolls you put in the microwave." Gary turned his attention to his other son, Josiah. "Joe, you behave yourself. Understand?"

Josiah nodded.

"And no talking back to your brother."

They shared a brief chuckle.

Gloria then moved in to smother Josiah with kisses and still he uttered not one word, but looked visibly embarrassed. Danius was on the verge of laughing at his brother's discomfort when he too was baptized in his mother's love.

"You two take care of yourselves and each other. We love you and we'll see you in a week."

"I love you too, Mom. Dad." Danius said while Josiah held up his hand, palm out, with the middle and ring fingers down, displaying the abbreviated sign for "I love you."

Anxious to get on the road, Gary and Gloria Todd peeled out almost as fast as they peeled in, leaving Danius and Josiah standing on the curb watching them drive off into the sunset. A few seconds ticked by before Danius broke the silence. "So Joe, are you looking forward to spending a whole week with your brother?"

Silence.

"I am." Danius said awkwardly. "We haven't done anything fun together since we took Alexandria to the county fair. Remember? That's where you…you know."

Josiah stuck his forefinger in his mouth and pretended to gag, then shrugged his shoulders as if there wasn't a thing he could do about it.

"Yeah." Danius said. "Well, let's go."

Danius arrived at the café an hour early, so he and Josiah took a seat at the smoothie bar. "I have to meet someone here at seven. So as long as we're here we might as well order something."

Josiah didn't respond but grabbed a menu and perused his options.

I can't even make small talk with him. It's going to be a long week. "Be creative." Mom had said. Well that's fine and dandy for someone who is creative, but Danius was not that person. He was always the type to deal with facts and figures. But they had to communicate somehow, so Danius plunged ahead. "If you see anything you want, just…point."

Josiah shot him a quick smile and nod.

Well that's a start anyway.

They spent an uneventful hour eating turkey-club sandwiches and sipping blueberry smoothies and *not* chatting while listening to a lone acoustic guitarist performing songs with strange titles such as: "Lilies In my Mind," "Let Me Be Your Cup of Water," and "The Love Vitamin." Then from the corner of his eye, Danius saw her coming towards him. He didn't want to analyze why he had to take a deep breath before turning to look at her, but he was glad he did because she would've taken his breath away.

Pearl walked towards Danius, or better yet, glided towards him in a cream colored sleeveless sundress and her hair pulled back. The light from the setting sun came in through the window and landed on her skin, giving Pearl a bronzed glow. She smiled and it was as if someone turned a light on somewhere.

There he was - as far as Pearl was concerned - the most handsome man on Earth. She'd thought about him almost constantly since yesterday. Here was a man in need of some serious fun. And as self-appointed ambassador of good, clean, fun, Pearl decided to make it her mission to see that he got it. Now she could lie to herself and say that that was the only reason that she wanted to spend time with him or she could be honest and admit that underneath all that stuffy business was a very unique and attractive individual who didn't seem to know he was attractive. Pearl decided to let the truth make her free. *I like him, God.* She prayed silently. *So what should I do about it?*

Then that still, small voice spoke into her heart the timeless words of Solomon, *"Trust in the Lord with all your heart and lean not unto your own understanding. In all your ways acknowledge him and he shall direct your paths.”*

Okay, she said. *It's all yours.* And with that, she approached him, smiling at her decision to leave Danius in the hands of God.

“Good   evening…Miss…uh…Pearl.”   Danius stammered.

“Well, look at you with no coat and tie on looking all relaxed.” she said. “I like it! Not that you don't look good in a suit, I'm just saying yesterday you looked a little uncomfortable; like you couldn't breathe. Still, I think you're the type who can pull off any style: business, casual, sporty, formal. Now this look you have going on says, ‘Business man who just got off from work.’ And who is the strong, silent type sitting next to you? He looks like you. Are you related?”

He shook his head at her swift change of subject. “Uh…yeah. This is my brother, Josiah. Josiah, this is Pearl, the woman who took my iPhone to South Carolina.”

“How do you do, Josiah? ‘Fire of the Lord’ oh, I do love that name.”

Josiah smiled and shyly looked away.

“You're a handsome one too. I think you're gonna grow up to be even more handsome than your brother.” Then turning to look Danius in the eye, Pearl added, “If such a thing is possible.”

What was Danius supposed to say to that? Luckily Josiah said it for him or rather signed it for him.

“You are beautiful.” Josiah signed.

Pearl smiled and signed back, “Thank you.”

“He's not deaf.” Danius said feeling the need to clarify the matter. “He's taking a vow of silence as my mother put it. It's just a game he's playing.”

Josiah turned to his brother and gave him a look that spoke volumes.

"Really? You know, when I was a kid, whenever I threw up, I would stop speaking for hours because I was afraid of throwing up again if I opened my mouth."

Danius, already tiring of the conversation said, "That's interesting and random. Well, Pearl if you'll give me back my iPhone, we'll be on our way."

"Oh, sure." she said. "It's in my backpack." Pearl turned as if to get it then remembered, "Which I left…in the van…that Patrick took to get tuned up."

"What?!" Danius stood and momentarily drew attention to him.

Pearl held both hands up and said, "Don't get upset. The shop's only ten minutes away and Patrick's bringing the van right back here so we can load up." Then turned to Josiah and explained, "Our band's going on tour."

Astonishment and admiration lit up Josiah's face.

"Pearl!" Danius said, demanding her attention. "When will this Patrick person be back?"

"About an hour."

"An hour?! What are we supposed to do in the meantime, sip coffee and talk about politics?"

Pear gave his question some thought. "Oh, I get it! 'Cause we're in a coffee shop, right? That's funny Danius; if not a little snippy and sarcastic. Don't worry. It won't be long. Patrick's very punctual. He's not one to doddle. Nope he is not a doddler; I can tell you that. There will be absolutely no doddling whatsoever. In fact I was just saying the other-"

"Fine. We'll wait." Danius sat back down in a huff.

Once again Pearl took pity on him. "I'm sorry, Danius. Are you mad?"

"Now why would I be mad?" he asked sarcastically. "It's just that the busses will stop running soon and we'll have to walk home.

"You'll do nothing of the kind. I will take you home. There now that's settled. Hey, while we're waiting, how'd you like to meet the rest of the band?

Josiah nodded emphatically while Danius tried to beg off but to no avail because no sooner than she asked the question, she was already beckoning them to come meet her "friends."

There at a round table on the other side of the café, sat three men and one woman in what appeared to be a serious conversation when Danius looked from a distance, but when he was close enough to hear what was being said, he furrowed his brow and tried to make sense of the whole thing. It seems they were playing a game where they took turns quoting cliché's. The trick was one person would quote a cliché and everyone else had to quote a similar one. So when Pearl, Danius and Josiah walked up to the table, they heard the young lady saying, "Don't bite off more than you can chew."

Then clockwise around the table, they heard;

"Never let your reach exceed you grasp."

"Never go to the grocery store when you're hungry."

"Your eyes are bigger than your stomach."

"That's a good one." said the others.

Pearl then interrupted the game to make the introductions. "Everybody I'd like you to meet Danius Todd, my newest and dearest friend. Remember him from yesterday?"

"Oh yeah. The iPhone guy." said one of them.

"And this is his younger brother Josiah. And now I'd like to introduce around the table on bass, Ms. Emily Cho."

"Cho!" repeated the guys. Emily smiled and nodded.

"Next. We have on drums, percussion, pots and pans, my very own cousin, Mr. Michael McClure." Michael was close enough to shake Danius's hand and give a cool head nod to Josiah.

"Next up, this man plays every instrument in the known galaxy including the triangle. Mr. Lewis Lewison."

"Yeah, my parents thought it would be funny." said Lewis.

"And it is." Pearl laughed. "And last but not least, on rhythm guitar and vocals, ladies and gentlemen give it up for Mr. Cary Stewart!"

"Thank you, Jacksonville!" shouted Cary.

"And my name is Pearl McClure. I play drums, I play keyboard, I play guitar but mostly they just make me sing and we are *Patiently Waiting.*

All together Emily threw up her rock fist, Cary gave a high pitched "Yeah," Michael beat on the table and said, "That's what's up!" and Lewis played air guitar while mimicking the sound of the notes.

Danius, shyly said, "Nice to meet you all." And Josiah simply smiled and nodded in agreement.

"You don't say much do you, boy?" Michael asked.

"He's a man of few words." said Pearl.

"I like him already." said Emily

"Then he probably wouldn't want to play our game." said Lewis.

Pearl turned to Josiah and asked, "What do you think, Hush? It's simple. One person quotes a famous saying or a cliché or a proverb or even a line from a movie and the others try and match it with one that sounds like it."

Josiah lifted his eyebrows, turned down his mouth and nodded, indicating he understood the rules. Michael pulled a chair up from another table and patted it. "Come on, Hush. Show me what you got."

Danius was about to explain the silly, pointless game Josiah was playing, but was interrupted by the scrape of the chair against the floor as Josiah sat down and gave a very intense look as if he were going to recite the *Gettysburg Address* or Martin Luther King's *I Have A Dream* speech. Josiah leaned forward, crossing his arms on the table and looked everyone at the table in the eyes then smiled and leaned back in his chair as if he'd said the most profound thing ever spoken. Danius rolled his eyes but everyone else stared at Josiah intensely. There was a moment of silence and then,

"Smile." said Pearl.

Then Michael said, "Smile and the whole world smiles with you."

Lewis said, "Smile because Jesus loves you."

Cary shrugged and asked, "A merry heart doeth good like a medicine?"

While Emily emphasized her point by hitting the table as she said, "Turn that frown upside down."

And Pearl concluded with, "Have a nice day."

Everyone laughed and gave high-fives to Josiah. "He's good." They said to each other.

Pearl looked at Danius and directed with her head, "He's deep." she said.

Danius sighed.

"You want to join in?" asked Pearl.

"No thank you. I think I'll just wait at the counter for your friend, Peter.

She smiled. "Oh, no. You're getting him confused with his brother."

"Who's brother?"

"Patrick's brother, Peter."

"What about Patrick's brother, Peter?"

"That's his name."

"Who?"

"Peter."

"Who's Peter?"

"Patrick's brother."

"Okay…so?"

"So nothing. I was just letting you know his name's not Peter. It's Patrick."

"You just said it *was* Peter."

"No! Peter is Patrick's brother. Patrick's name is Patrick, not Peter."

Danius shook his head in frustration. "Look, all I want to know is will he be here soon with the van?"

"No. He lives in Philadelphia."

"Who does?"

"Peter."

"Not him, his brother!"

"Which one, Patrick?"

"Yes!"

"Oh, he's lived here for years."

"I…" Danius rubbed his forehead and closed his eyes. "I think I have a headache."

"I've got some aspirin. Oh, but I left it in the van. Don't worry though. He'll be here soon.

"Who, Patrick or Peter?" Danius asked sarcastically, now rubbing his temples.

"Patrick."

"Thank you."

Everyone at the table clapped when Pearl and Danius finished their conversation. Danius looked at Pearl. She only shrugged her shoulders, not knowing why they clapped for them.

After an hour and a half, *Patrick* finally showed up and as promised, Pearl drove Danius and Josiah home. On the way, Pearl had a rousing one-sided conversation with Josiah to Danius's amazement and annoyance. It amazed him that Pearl had such a way with people, she could communicate with an adolescent who refused to speak. It annoyed him that he couldn't do it. And Josiah was *his* brother. Danius was right in the middle of sulking when his cell rang. "Yes!" He answered slightly embittered.

"Where have you been? I've been calling your cell phone all day." said the perturbed Alexandria.

"Oh…Alexandria…hello…uh…well…I'm sorry…I didn't have my phone today…it was out of town."

"What? You mean *you* were out of town?

"No. My phone was."

"How can your phone be out of town without you? That doesn't make sense."

"Yeah. It…it doesn't. You see...well…it's a long story."

"But funny when you think about it, right? Pearl said to Josiah who smiled and nodded.

"Who was that?" Alexandria demanded.

Danius fumbled, mumbled and stumbled through his explanation. "Just…uh…someone giving me a ride home."

"It sounded like a girl."

"Well she's a girl, but she's not a *girl*."

"No," said Pearl. "But I am a *girl*."

Danius covered the phone with his other hand and said, "I know you're a girl. She doesn't know that you're a girl. Well, she knows you're a girl, but she doesn't know that you're *just* a girl.

"As long as everybody understands that I am a girl, it's all right with me."

"Of course. No one's doubting your girl…hood…I mean…Oh, would you please just keep you voice down?" He put the phone back to his ear.

"Is she upset with you? I feel like it's my fault. Why don't I talk to her?" Pearl reached for the phone, but Danius quickly moved it out of her reach.

"No!" he said. "Please be quiet."

"What?" said Alexandria in his ear.

"Oh! No not you. I…uh."

"Danius Todd, what is going on? Who is that girl?"

"No one. I just told you she's not a *girl*. She's just a friend who's driving Josiah and me home. That's all."

"I thought I knew all of your friends. Who is she?"

"She's…" Danius looked over at Pearl who kept her eyes on the road. Her lips were slightly turned upward as if she were on the verge of smiling at any second. "…hard to explain."

And there was that smile.

"Fine.   Maybe you can try explaining her tomorrow."

"Tomorrow?"

"Yes. That's what I called to talk about. I decided that just because your brother is with us doesn't mean our weekend has to be ruined. The Fine Arts Museum has a new exhibit and I thought we could go tomorrow, after you get off work. Then on, Saturday, my father would like to see you. He wants to discuss your future. He just bought his partner at the firm out and now that he has full control, he's cleaning house, so to speak, there may be an opening for you."

"Oh, well that sounds…great." said Danius trying to sound more enthusiastic than he really was. "What about Josiah?"

"Well if you have to bring him, you have to bring him. Just make sure he stays out of the way when you meet Daddy and please make sure Josiah doesn't eat or drink anything red."

"Yes. I'll try. Well, I'll see you tomorrow then. Have a good night Alexandria."

Alexandria didn't even say goodbye before she hung up, which left Danius staring at the phone for a second.

"Well, Josiah." he said. "Good news. Alexandria has invited us to the Fine Arts Museum and then to her house. It's pretty big and you can meet her parents. Oh and she has a dog named Kitten. Isn't that funny?" Danius chuckled. "He's a little poodle."

Josiah gave Danius the same look he gives his mother whenever she makes him take medicine or play with the kid down the street who smells like cheese. Then he leaned back in his seat, folded his arms and gave a heavy sigh.

Josiah's attitude and Danius's What-Am-I-Supposed-To-Do expression was not lost on Pearl. She felt sorry for the brothers especially for Danius who now seemed to be looking at his iPhone as if it held the answer to his problems.

"Well," she said "Sounds like you guys have a full weekend ahead of you: The museum, meeting parents, a confused dog…" Josiah chuckled out loud at that. "Too bad for me, I guess. I wanted to invite you to come with us on tour. It's gonna be hectic but great. I'm talking four different venues in one day, ending at a skate park."

Josiah leaned forward again as Pearl continued. "Then Saturday we got a nursing home gig and a half-way house. Then we'll drive back up the coast and I guess we'll see you at Frederick's."

"Oh, no!" said Danius. "I completely forgot about Mr. Maxwell!" He buried his head in his hands. "What am I going to do? I'll just have to reschedule with Mr. Maxwell. Oh, but I can't do that. It's for my job."

"Maybe you could persuade your girlfriend to come with you or if not, maybe you could reschedule the Fine Arts Museum." Pearl had her eyes on the road, but she could feel Danius's Are-You-Kidding-Me stare. "I'm just gonna retract that last statement." she said "because something tells me Alexandria doesn't like being rescheduled."

Josiah scoffed in the back seat and shook his head. Danius looked back at him and then to Pearl and then out the window for the rest of the ride home.

When Pearl pulled into the complex, Josiah tapped Danius on the shoulder and pointed to the car parked next to them.

"Oh." said Danius "Mom left her car for us. Great. Well um…thank you, Pearl, for the ride home." He shifted nervously in his seat.

"It was my pleasure, Mr. Todd. I hope to see you at Frederick's and if not, I hope to see you soon." The sincere look in her eyes and the tone of her voice reminded Danius of something warm on a cold day and he felt it all the way down to his toes.

She turned toward the back seat where Josiah was and said in a much lighter tone, "Josiah, you and me are friends from now on. I wish you were coming with us, but you'll have a good time with your brother. Will you come by and see me at the café? I'm there all the time."

Josiah nodded then shared a fist bump with Pearl before jumping out of the van. That left Pearl and Danius alone in the van momentarily. There was about two seconds of awkward silence before Pearl said, "Goodnight, Danius."

For a moment it looked as if Danius was going to say something but then he looked down and finally said goodnight, then quickly got out of the van.

"Oh, hey." she said before he closed the door. "You and me…friends from now on."

He would've replied to her, but he couldn't get any words around the lump in his throat. So he gave her an awkward smile and nodded before closing the van door.

He carried that warm feeling with him to bed that night, but now he had a problem. He kept telling himself that he had his iPhone back and after this weekend he really wouldn't have a reason to see Pearl anymore. He could get back to his normal life with his normal schedule and his normal girlfriend. He should be happy, right? But as disruptive and unsettling as Pearl McClure was, the thought of never seeing her again was even more unsettling and that was the problem.

He was determined to put all of this out of his mind and put it all behind him. He concentrated on Alexandria, his girlfriend of nearly four years. She was the woman of his dreams - she said so herself - and yet when Danius finally drifted off to sleep, it wasn't *Alexandria's* face he was picturing, nor was it *her* voice that he played over and over again in his mind.

And it wasn't Alexandria's phone call that woke him at 4:30 in the morning. Groggily, he answered on the fourth ring. "Hello?"

"Hi, Danius. It's Pearl. Did I wake you?"

Still thinking he was dreaming, Danius relaxed against his pillow and sighed at the pleasant sound of her voice. "Oh, Pearl…PEARL!" He sat up so fast he made himself dizzy. "What are you…how'd you get my number? Do you know what time it is?"

"Well I called my phone from your phone while I was in South Carolina. Then I programmed my number into your phone. By the way, you have some really nice ring tones. You should use 'em. And it is 4:32. Anyway, I was just calling to let you know we made it to West Palm Beach safely and that your brother stowed away in our van, but he's all right. If you want to come and get him, I'll give you directions. If not, I'll watch out for him and we'll just meet you at Mrs. Maxwell's birthday party."

Danius was fully awake now, but it still took him a moment before he was able to say, "My brother did what?"

The Adventure Begins

"How could he have snuck out?" Danius asked no one in particular. After Pearl's phone call, it only took an hour for Danius to dress, splash water on his face, gas up his mother's car and buy a large cup of the strongest, black coffee he could find. He didn't even like coffee. Now he was traveling down Interstate 95 alone during the darkest part of the night. "How could I not have heard him?"

Danius replayed everything that had happened after Pearl had dropped them off. He'd asked Josiah if he was hungry, Josiah shook his head no. Josiah pulled out a deck of playing cards from his back-pack and gestured to Danius if he wanted to play. Danius declined, saying something about having to get up early in the morning to go to work, leaving Josiah alone in the living room to play solitaire. That was the last time he saw him before shutting his bedroom door and going to sleep.

"I shut the door." Danius never shut his bedroom door, not even on those rare occasions when a friend would stay over. He closed his bedroom door out of habit when it came to his brother. Being fourteen years older than Josiah, Danius had little in common with him and had very little patience when it came to spending time with him. When he lived at home, Josiah would always be in his room asking him to play a game or watch a movie with him or go outside and watch him do a trick on his skateboard. Sometimes Josiah would come into Danius's room for no particular reason and sit on the bed or on the floor, make noise and bother things which annoyed Danius to no end, so he would close and lock his door to keep out his annoying little brother.

And now his annoying little brother had taken it upon himself to run away from home, on Danius's watch, of all people. The thought of this infuriated Danius. Didn't Josiah realize that Danius had obligations such as work, keeping Alexandria happy, meeting with her father, meeting with Mr. Maxwell? Didn't Pearl realize that to drop everything to drive to West Palm Beach to bring back his wayward brother was a real sacrifice? Maybe she and her band mates could slack off, being musicians and all, but he had goals and those goals required focus and diligence. This whole situation was terribly inconvenient and he was going to make sure Pearl and Josiah knew it.

Dude, where's your car?

When Pearl first noticed Josiah underneath the back seat of the van she was shocked and furious and she'd let him know about it, too. But now that she'd had a chance to think about it, she really could kiss the darling boy for what he'd done. This meant that she would see Danius again. She was too giddy for words. Oh, Josiah was not off the hook, by no means, but Pearl thought that perhaps between the two of them they could get Danius to loosen up. It would take some doing because he sounded as if he could spit nails when she spoke to him on the phone.

It would take Danius at least three hours to get to them so Pearl and the others decided to get some sleep at a motel near the place where they would perform first. By 9am the sound of Michael Jackson's "Wanna Be Startin' Somethin'" on her cell phone startled her awake. It was Danius calling for directions to the motel. Fifteen minutes later she saw from the window a blue Buick skidding to a stop in the dusty parking lot creating a dust cloud. "Ooh, he's mad." Pearl said out loud as Danius struggled with the seat belt and the door trying to get out of the car.

A dirty, disheveled looking man then walked up to Danius, apparently asking for a hand out. Danius shook his head and tried to walk around him. The man tried once more to ask for help and again Danius refused him, walking purposefully to Pearl's door. Pearl swung the door open before he even had a chance to knock.

"Good morning, Danius. It's good to see you again." she said quietly, trying not to wake Emily who was rooming with her.

"Where is he?" asked the fire-breathing Danius. He made a move to step inside Pearl's room but she placed both hands on his chest to stop him.

"Wow! Do you work out?" she asked.

"Pearl!"

"I'm just saying, you're kind of solid there. Nice."

"Where's my brother?"

"He's in the next room with the guys, but Danius, listen to me for one second. Right now you're madder than a bear with a thorn in his paw and you have every right to be. But why don't you just let him sleep? It'll give you a chance to calm down, that way when he wakes up you can rip him a new one with a cool head."

"I don't have time for that." Danius said as he stomped over to the next room and began pounding on the door. "I have to get back on the road so I can salvage what's left of my day."

"You can't drive upset like this. You're too distracted. You could get in an accident and I'd never forgive myself for letting you go."

"Well that's just too bad." he said. Danius pounded again, this time yelling Josiah's name. Patrick opened the door and Danius didn't even wait to be let in. He marched right up to the fold-out couch where Josiah was sleeping and snatched the covers off of him.

Groggy and disoriented, Josiah stared up at Danius trying to make sense of the whole situation. Suddenly everyone was awake and talking at the same time.

"What were you thinking?!" Danius yelled.

"Wait a minute. Just calm down." said Patrick.

"How you just gon' rip the covers off like that?" said Michael who was sharing the fold out with Josiah.

"I think we'll all feel better if we just sit down, have some breakfast and talk this thing out." said Lewis, ever the diplomat.

Pearl, who'd followed Danius in trying to reason with him, was now trying to get his attention by calling his name repeatedly. Finally she just grabbed his face in both hands, smushing his cheeks so that he looked like a fish. "Danius!"

Danius pushed her hands away, "What Pearl?! What is it? What do you want?"

She grabbed his shoulders and said, "Just to tell you your Buick is heading southbound on Broad Street."

"What!"

Then everybody scurried like roaches from the room and into the parking lot.

"Oh, no!" Danius screamed as he watched his mom's car move further and further away. "No! Hey, come back! That's my mom's car!" Then he looked up to the sky and screamed, "What else can happen?!"

"Hey, 'morning guys. What's going on?"

Everyone turned to look at Emily who had just woken up.

Patiently Waiting

There in the middle of the road, stood Danius unblinking, staring after the car that had left his sight nearly two minutes ago. He felt sort of light weight and heavy at the same time. Somewhere in his mind he knew he should get out of the street before an 18-wheeler hit him, but he couldn't move.

Everyone stared silently at Danius, afraid to go near him until at last Pearl carefully approached him and ever so lightly placed a hand on his arm. "Danius, you okay?"

"That was my mom's brand new Buick Regal." Danius said, still staring ahead. "It was her birthday present from Dad."

"Oh, I'm sorry." said Pearl.

"They only just started making those again in the U.S. after seven years. He bought the one off the show-room floor."

"Really?" asked Pearl as she slowly began to walk him towards a bench outside the motel. "Let's get out of the road, okay? Then you can tell me all about it."

"It's blue. That's her favorite color." he said as he was being pulled.

"I know, sweetie. Just come over here and sit down. It'll be all right."

"Blue is a nice color, don't you think?"

Danius sat down in a defeated slump. After everyone had gathered around him, Cary suggested slapping him to snap him out of it. Josiah raised his arm in a back-handed fashion and moved to slap his brother when Pearl stopped him. "No, no. He'll be all right. Just give him a few minutes."

Danius slowly regained his sanity as Patrick called the police and explained the situation. He knew he was coming around when Pearl's voice was no longer a buzzing sound in his ear and he could actually understand what she was saying.

"Danius?" she said. "I don't want you to worry. Patrick called the police and we're all going to help you work this out, okay? Blink twice if you understand."

He turned toward her with a deadpan expression and blinked twice.

"He blinked!" Pearl announced to the others. They all congratulated Danius on his speedy recovery.

The Police came and went and by that time he was pretty well back to normal…almost.

When Josiah happened across his path he snapped, but this time with anger. "Hey!" he yelled. "I hope you're satisfied. Because of you I'm missing work and everything else I had planned for today is ruined. And now mom's car has been stolen. This is the mess they've got to come home to. What were you thinking running away like that with people you don't even know? Do you have any idea how dangerous that is?"

Josiah defiantly folded his arms and refused to speak.

"I'm talking to you." Danius demanded.

Josiah made a move to walk away, but Danius grabbed his arm and swung him back around to face him.

"Don't you pull that 'mute' crap with me. I demand an explanation. Talk!"

It took all of Josiah's might to push his brother away from him. "What for?!" He shouted and everyone turned to look at him for these were the first words Pearl and the others had heard him speak. "You never listen to me anyway. Why should I tell you anything? You don't care about me. All you care about is your stupid job and your stupid schedule and your stupid girlfriend. She doesn't even like you, Danius; which shows how stupid you are." Josiah ran back to the motel room and slammed the door shut.

"Dang!" said the band in a stage whisper.

Danius started to go after him, but Pearl stopped him.

"Danius wait. Why don't you give him some time to calm down?"

"And why don't you mind your own business? This is between me and my brother. We wouldn't even be in this mess if it wasn't for you."

"What did I do?"

Danius put one hand on his hip and waved in a mock feminine gesture. "Oh Josiah, I wish you were coming with us."

"What was that? Was that supposed to me?"

"That is exactly what you said to him last night. Don't deny it."

"Yeah, but I didn't tell him to hide in our van, did I? How in the world did this suddenly become my fault?"

"Well Pearl, look where I am after two days of knowing *you*."

"Dang!" whispered the band.

Pearl gave him the universal Oh-No-You-Didn't look and said, "Listen, I know you're upset, but blaming me and snapping at people isn't going help matters. For one thing, *you're* the one who needs a ride home. Now you didn't listen to me before. Will you please listen to me now? Give yourself and Josiah a chance to calm down. Think about what he just told you. And then go and talk *to* him, not yell *at* him.

He paced in front of her, wanting to argue the point further, to tell her he didn't need her to give him a ride home, he was doing just fine before he met her, and to tell her to take a hike, but there was no use. He gave a sigh of concession. She made sense. It irked him, but she made sense. "You're right. I'm sorry."

Pearl flashed a forgiving smile. "Why don't we go to the diner across the street and have some breakfast?"

"I couldn't eat anything."

"Well I can. Being right always makes me hungry." Then she took him by the hand and led him across the street.

The *Patiently Waiting* band, all except Emily, surrounded Danius as he sat in a booth and stared out at the motel across the street where his brother had opted to stay. Pearl sat across from him. Her hands were resting inches away from his and she ached to reach out to comfort him.

"Danius he's all right. Emily's with him, keeping him company. And when I took him his breakfast just now he was sitting down watching TV Land."

"What's on?" asked her cousin, Michael.

"*Good Times* marathon." she said.

"The marathon?" Michael and the rest of the band gathered their food, paid their checks, asked for to-go boxes and were out of there and back across the street in under two minutes.

"Why didn't you go with them?" Danius asked Pearl.

"I have the complete box-set at home; the Dy-no-mite edition." she said with a smile.

"Oh." he said and resumed his staring.

"Are you gonna be okay?"

Danius shook his head and shrugged his shoulders. "He wanted to play cards last night and I blew him off. I complained about having to watch him for a whole week. Alexandria doesn't like to be around him and he knows it. And I had the nerve to blame him for all this."

"Hey, he's not without fault. No matter what you did or didn't do, he still shouldn't have run off like that."

"Yeah, well who wouldn't run away from the world's most rotten brother?"

"You can't be all that rotten. You did drive all the way here and you feel bad about what you said. You love him. I think he knows that. But I get the feeling he thinks you don't *like* him. I mean, he's your brother and you love him 'cause you have to, but do you *care* about him? Are you interested in him as a person?"

Pearl hadn't expected him to answer the question, only think about it.

"I guess not." he whispered. "But only because I never really thought of him as his own person. He's always just been 'my little brother.' We've never been close. I always thought it was our age difference, but...it was me all along. I never let him get close. It's probably too late now."

Pearl shook her head. "As long as there is breath in the body, it's never too late."

For the first time since they'd met two days ago, Danius really looked at Pearl and allowed himself to drink in her lovely features: her coffee colored eyes, her smooth, dark skin, a small scar underneath her right eyebrow and what some would call a beauty mole underneath her bottom lip–something a supermodel would probably kill for--and her mouth, so enticing, he had to look away.

"How did you get to be so wise?" he asked.

"*Full House* marathon...was on last week."

Danius smiled, genuinely, for the first time since he'd met Pearl. It made her heart beat just a little bit faster. "Nah, man. I told you. I have a brother and sister."

"And they treated you the way I treated Josiah?"

"Other way around." Pearl looked away briefly as if she saw something she'd rather not see.

"You?"

Pearl nodded.

"I find that hard to believe. You're...I don't know...nice...really nice. I can't imagine you ever doing anything like that."

Pearl shrugged. "I've had my moments. Everyone does."

So she wasn't one dimensional. She wasn't perpetually perky. Pearl McClure actually had depth. She had layers. She had short-comings. Danius didn't know why that interested him, but it did.

"Why don't you go over and see if Josiah is ready to talk?" she said.

Danius nodded and stood to leave, when he and Pearl both noticed their fingers laced together.

"Wow." said Pearl. "How did that happen?" There was a moment of silence before Danius let her hand go and awkwardly made his way out of the restaurant.

Danius was ready to make amends with his brother and walked back to the motel to do just that, not wanting to put it off any longer. But when he walked into the room and asked Josiah if he could speak to him he was shushed seven times over.

"This is the episode where James dies and they're just getting back from the funeral." whispered Michael.

Then at the appropriate moment, everyone on one accord mimed Ester Rolle's famous, grief-stricken, heart-wrenching line from that episode.

Two episodes later as the band was packing to go to their first gig, Danius finally found a private moment to talk to Josiah. He found him throwing a tennis ball up against the wall and catching it. "Joe?"

Josiah didn't answer but he did turn his attention toward Danius.

"I just want to say, first of all, that I'm glad you're all right. You were wrong for running away, but the band has taken good care of you and I'm very grateful. And I'm sorry for making you feel like I didn't care about you, because I do care about *you* very much. I...love you."

Josiah smiled at that last part. It was the first time he'd ever heard those words from his brother. "I'm sorry I ran away and I'm sorry for calling you stupid…and your job and your schedule."

"And Alexandria?"

Josiah took this moment to examine his tennis ball with its roundness and its lovely neon green color.

"Josiah!"

"Okay. I'm sorry I called her stupid, but what I said about her not liking you is the truth."

"What makes you think she doesn't like me? She's been my girlfriend for four years."

"Do you hear the way she talks to you? I think she just likes having someone to boss around and you let her. I didn't want to spend the week watching you get jerked around by her. I wanted to have fun." Josiah turned to watch the guys load the rest of their things in the van. Danius turned and did the same.

This tight-knit group of four guys and two girls seemed to have fun no matter where they were or what they were doing. Even now while loading the van-a seemingly menial chore-they were talking and laughing together; happy just being in each other's company. When was the last time Danius had ever felt that way? The closest friend he'd ever had moved away after high school and he hadn't seen or heard from him since. He had a few acquaintances he'd met through Alexandria and he considered them friends but they didn't hang out or joke around the way Pearl and her friends did; the way they were doing now. To tell the truth, *his* friends were a little on the bland side.

"Come on." He put his arm around Josiah as they walked back to the van.

"Danius? Mom and Dad are gonna kill me when they get home, aren't they?"

"Yes, I think so. But don't worry. You won't die alone. I'm the idiot who left the keys in the ignition with the doors unlocked."

"Wow! Thanks."

When the band was all packed and ready to go they insisted Danius and Josiah go with them on this mini-tour of theirs. Danius tried explaining to them that Alexandria could wire him some money so he and Josiah could take a bus home seeing as how he left in such a hurry, all he grabbed was his wallet and the cash that was on his dresser, leaving his debit card that he only carried with him when he went grocery shopping. But Pearl would hear none of it. She insisted that it would work out better this way in the long run. It wouldn't cost him a thing and they were all going to the Maxwell party anyway, so why not come along and be a "roadie."

"We've never had roadies before. This will be fun." she said. "Now Danius, I know what you're thinking. You're probably worried about what your girlfriend's going to think. Well, if I know anything about women, it's that we are very understanding, very loving, very forgiving; unless we're selfish and spoiled and think only of ourselves. But I'm sure your girlfriend is nothing like that. I'm sure she's not the type who'll rant and rave about how inconvenient this whole thing is, knowing that the man she loves or likes a little bit, at least, is stranded somewhere in south Florida. No. I'm sure she'll understand when you explain it to her and everything's going to be all right. Now I want you to put this whole thing out of your mind and come ride with us."

That was all the prompting Josiah needed. He jumped in the van and claimed a seat without so much as a backward glance. It took Danius a little bit longer to decide, though. He didn't relish having to explain to Alexandria why he wouldn't be home in time to meet her and her father. He was not looking forward to the clipped words and the icy tone of voice that accompanied her attitude whenever she was the least bit perturbed. She'd simply have to understand, as Danius himself had only just begun to learn, that some things just can't be helped: like runaway kids and auto theft and Pearl McClure. It seemed like the longer he stayed in the company of Pearl, the stranger his life became, but she was a flame and he was a moth. So reluctantly or maybe not so reluctantly, he got into the van.

The van was a tricked-out G20 Van Dura Camper, a character in itself. It had almost as much personality as the band members who occupied it. The exterior was black with red stripes. The massive interior was tan with black and red accents throughout. There was a specially made compartment that housed the amplifiers and most of Michael's drum kit. All other equipment and instruments were kept in overhead compartments or on the roof rack. There was a mini-fridge and a mini-flat screen T.V. overhead. But what gave the van its character were the pictures; wall to wall pictures of the band either together at different venues or apart, with family members or fans. Somehow the van itself seemed to sneak into most of the pictures like one of those photo-bombers you see all throughout a school year book.

Danius chose a seat next to Josiah and was about to buckle up when Pearl suggested they pray first before heading out.

"All right, everybody grab a hand. Heavenly Father, thank you for another day to live for you and serve you. Guide us, Lord and let your will be done on this trip. Show us how to be a blessing to all we come in contact with. And, Lord I thank you for our two new friends. Please watch over them and protect them. And may they put their trust in you and allow you to direct their paths always. In the name of our Lord, Jesus, amen.”

Amens echoed throughout the van, but Danius stayed silent. It was just a simple prayer of thanksgiving and protection, but something about it grabbed at his heart and rendered him speechless. Once again he wondered when was it that he stopped praying for God’s protection and guidance. For that matter, when did he stop praying, period?

He believed in God. He went to church every Sunday and men’s Bible study with Alexandria’s father, but there was still something missing. He didn’t even think to pray for Josiah when he found out the boy had run away. What was wrong with him? He’d asked himself this question numerous times before but he just never seemed to have time to answer it.

“Well, your plans have changed. You have nothing but time right now.” A voice out of nowhere spoke to him. Not so much a voice he could hear, but a voice he could, sort of, feel inside. He heard Patrick say it would take about an hour to get to where they were going, so Danius settled in, turned his attention to the passing scenery and thought about what that Voice said.

Joe Verses the Half Pipe

Danius didn't know what to expect from a music tour, but what he saw was a pleasant surprise. *Patiently Waiting* was the featured band first at the grand opening of a *Countrified Cookin'* restaurant, then at a children's hospital. Next they opened for a big name band at a rock festival that migrated to a skate park's block party.

Each performance seemed to be tailor made to the venue itself. At the restaurant, Lewis actually played a fiddle and Pearl sang an angry country song about what a woman did to the car of the man who cheated on her. At the children's hospital, they played softly on their acoustic instruments. The highlight was Pearl reading a children's book with Lewis and Cary accompanying her on their guitars for effect. But they exploded on the stages of the rock festival and the skate park with their own high-energy, original music including the song Danius had heard when he first met Pearl. They were truly amazing.

In between performances, Danius got to know each member on a more personal level and was set straight on a few things. For instance, he'd assumed, at first, they were a bunch of slackers who used "music" as an excuse not to grow up and get real jobs, but in actuality they all had "real" jobs. Emily was a nurse in training, Lewis taught music appreciation and general math at a middle school, Michael worked as a teller in a credit-union, Patrick and Cary both worked as groundwater inspectors for the city. And Pearl owned and managed the café where they all hung out.

Before Danius knew any of this, he'd, on more than one occasion, been tempted to chastise them for bumming around a café waiting for the next big gig like a bunch of beatniks from the 50s. He hated seeing able-bodied, grown men and women not doing anything and getting by when he had to work hard and pinch pennies and was still only just making his rent. But these people seemed to have it together and if Danius were honest with himself, he would have to admit he was a little jealous.

When the concert was over, the skate park opened to the public and hundreds of young people invaded the place like ants at a picnic. The band stowed their gear and came back to watch the skaters. Josiah took off with Patrick and Michael while Cary, Emily and Lewis took off in the opposite direction, leaving Danius and Pearl alone or as alone as two people could be in a crowded skate park.

"So Danius, tell me about yourself. Like, what do you do?" Pearl asked. She nearly had to scream in order to be heard over the noise.

"I'm an instruction writer."

"An instruction writer? So you're the guy who writes 'Shake well' on orange juice cartons? That's cool."

"It's a little more complicated than that." Danius said as they walked up the steps of a set of bleachers. They sat on the very top row, away from the crowd, where it was quieter. "For instance, Mr. Maxwell has created a new computer software program for office buildings all across the country. It's quite complex. It includes office automation, multimedia and telecommunications. He doesn't have time to teach the IT specialists how it's done, so that's where I come in."

"What other things do you write instructions for?"

"Oh, just about anything. You name it."

"Wow! You must know how to do a lot of stuff, if you can tell someone how to do it."

"Not really…*those who can't, teach*, as the saying goes."

Pearl thought she saw a sad look on his face. "I take it Instruction Writing is not your cup of tea?" she asked.

"It's an okay job, I guess. I've been doing it since college as a way to help pay for school."

"What were you studying?"

Danius was a little embarrassed to say and it showed in his shy smile. "Chemistry, Earth Space Science, Biology, Astronomy..."

"Oh, so you wanted to be a mad scientist."

"Mad science *teacher* to be exact. Don't laugh. But I use to want to be just like Bill Nye The Science Guy."

"Are you kidding me? Man, I used to love his show!"

"Yeah? Me too. And I got to meet him in person when I was in the fifth grade. He made science fun to learn and it looked like he was having fun teaching it. From then on that's what I wanted to do. I was pretty good at it, too. You know, I would tutor the other kids and pretty soon they would ask me to help them with other subjects like, math and reading and..." Danius let the sentence drop and shook his head.

"You know what? I can totally see you in a lab coat and glasses and weird hair. So what happened?"

"Well I could never support Al...uh...a wife and kids on a teacher's salary. I mean have you seen what teachers make?"

Pearl didn't answer that. She thought his wanting to be a teacher was wonderful, but she understood what he meant. This Alexandria chick must be high maintenance. "So if you don't want to be an instruction writer and you don't want to be a teacher, what do you want to do?"

"I'm seriously considering going into law."

For a brief moment, Pearl saw that sad look cross his face once more, but it was quickly replaced by a strained smile. She thought it would be best to lighten the mood.

"Well, I wish you all the best. But for the time being, instruction writing sounds like an interesting job.

I've always wondered about interesting jobs like that, you know like, who designs decorative toilet paper…and why? Who's the guy that recites all the side effects on those prescription drug commercials? Is there a person who puts aglets on the ends of shoe laces or does a machine do it? Who writes the fortunes in fortune cookies? And the person who works at a water treatment facility, who literally has to take people's crap all day; who's that guy? Better yet, who's the wife of that guy?"

Danius laughed so hard and for so long, his eyes watered. This was the first time Pearl had heard him laugh-truly laugh-and it was lovely.

"I mean she's the one who has to kiss him when he comes home, right? God bless her." she said, causing another round of laughter.

"I haven't laughed like that since…gosh, I don't know when." Danius said, when was able to speak again. "Pearl you're so…well…let's just say, I've never met anyone quite like you."

"Oh, I'm just your average girl."

"I beg to differ. You are an anomaly."

"An anomaly: A deviation from the normal or common order, form, or rule. So what you're saying is I'm not normal. That's all right. I'm going to take that as a compliment."

"See, that right there; what you just did? Why do you know the exact definition of anomaly? And why do you know the name of the plastic thing at the end of a shoe lace?"

They both laughed.
Pearl shrugged her shoulders. "Well, I like to read and when I come across a word I don't know, I look it up. Growing up, I lived with my older cousins and they used to tease me about always having my face buried in a book. But my aunt would tell me, 'Keep it up, child. Those big words will come in handy someday. Now I'm going to let

you in on a little secret, so don't tell anyone what I'm about to tell you."

"All right."

"Now I know I give off this air of cool, laid-back, rocker chick, but as cool as I am, as adventurous and fun-loving as I am, I'm also…a closet nerd."

"You're kidding."

"No, it's true. I'm all about $E=MC^2$."

Danius shook his head. He didn't agree with her statement. She was incredibly smart, but she was no nerd. "No, you're…something else."

She smiled and that warm feeling he now associated with Pearl wrapped itself around him like a blanket and when he looked up at her, he saw for a moment his feelings reflected in her eyes.

"I'm glad you decided to come with us." Pearl said.

He looked away. "I didn't have much of a choice, did I?" He tried to make it sound cold; to remind Pearl… and himself that there was nothing-nor could there ever be anything-between them. He could tell she wasn't buying it, neither was he at the moment.

"Yes you did."

It was true. He could've called Alexandria and asked for the money like he'd suggested, but the plain truth was he liked being around Pearl. She was strange and fun and kind-hearted and so incredibly attractive he couldn't have looked away if he wanted to.

"Yes I did." He timidly admitted.

She nodded. "Do you want to tell me why you decided to come with us?"

Danius took a breath as if he were about to speak but shook his head instead.

He was so incredibly attractive, Pearl couldn't have looked away if she wanted to. She watched as he stared, fixated on her mouth, like a hungry man at a buffet.

Whether she moved closer or he did, Pearl didn't know, but there wasn't a whole lot of space left between them when they heard someone yell, "Hey, look at that kid!"

Startled, they turned to see what the commotion was about. There was a boy-all of twelve-landing tricks on a vert ramp that would rival any man twice his size and age. Then Pearl stood up fast when she recognized who he was. "It's Josiah!"

"My brother?" asked Danius.

Pearl grabbed Danius's hand and practically dragged him down the steps, through the crowd and up to the gate that surrounded the ramps. They saw Patrick and the others and they pressed their way through the crowd to stand with them.

"Yo, did you see your brother nail that 360?" asked Michael. "That kid is sick!"

Danius did a double take, not knowing what Michael meant by *sick*. He heard other people in the crowd saying it too along with words like *wicked* and *insane*. They were all staring in awe of Josiah's skateboarding skills and Danius soon came to realize that *sick* meant simply *amazing*.

It was a good thing Michael was standing next to him acting as sports announcer because Danius had no clue what Josiah was doing or what to call his mid-air acrobatics. Michael gave him a play by play description of each trick. Josiah did what was called a Backside Air, an Air Walk, a Frontside Air then something called a Stalefish and finished with a Back flip causing the crowd to go wild and Michael to grab Danius by the shirt and scream, "Back flip! Back flip! He nailed it!"

Then somewhere an air horn blew and Josiah "dropped in" on one side of the half pipe and rode up the other side. In mid-air, he grabbed his board and landed with his feet on the deck. Amid the deafening roar of the crowd, Danius stood, his chest swelling with pride.

When Josiah finally made it through the congratulatory crowd, the *Patiently Waiting* band attacked him. The guys slapped him on the back and high-fived him while the girls covered him with hugs and kisses. Danius was last in line. He rested his hands on Josiah's shoulders and bent down to his eye-level. "Joe…that was incredible! I had no idea you were that good."

Josiah gave him a very humble "Thanks" And for the first time in years Danius hugged his little brother.

As Pearl looked on, she gave a silent prayer of thanks to God for the day and for the brothers who were becoming friends.

Science, Attraction and Other Random Things

The band and their two new friends took a tour of the skate park and found an arcade attached to a pizzeria. The place was packed like a sardine can. They all ordered individual slices and soda from a menu that boasted a special called the Stuff Your Face; one huge carnivorous, deep-dish slice of pizza piled high with toppings that only the brave would pick up and eat with his hands. Patrick treated Josiah to this artery-clogging delicacy in honor of his heroic feats of daring on the vert ramp.

"You could feed a small, Ethiopian family for three days with that thing." said Pearl.

Josiah opened his mouth as wide as it could go and took his first bite. "I'm confused. Does that mean you *want* me to eat it or you *don't* want me to eat it? My mom says stuff like that when she *wants* me to eat everything on my plate.

They all laughed.

"Joe." Pearl said. "I'll pay good money to see you eat that whole thing."

"Deal."

"Hey, let me get in on that." said Michael.

The rest of the band put their money up as Michael laid down the terms. "All right lil' homie. If you eat the entire thing in thirty minutes, the money is yours. If not, you have to wash and wax the Van Dura."

"Bring it on." said Josiah.

"Oh, it's being brought to you by the letter *I* 'cause *I* don't think you can do it."

Josiah took another big bite, pointed to his mouth and gloated to his new friends, "All day, baby. All day."

"Great." said Danius. "On top of everything else, I'm going to have to get his stomach pumped."

Pearl laughed. "Don't worry. I have antacids in my purse, for moments like these."

"Moments like these." Danius shook his head. "I suppose I'd be the stick-in-the-mud if I put a stop to this crazy bet. You all do this sort of thing all the time?"

"Only when we get together. Why? What do you do for fun?"

He started to speak but Josiah cut in with a mouth full of pizza. "Read science magazines and watch the Discovery Channel."

"Science?" asked Cary with genuine interest.

"Science?" asked Michael with genuine aversion.

Pearl gestured toward Danius. "Oh, heck yeah! This man is not just a pretty face, y'all. He's got brains. In fact, personally, I think he'd make a good teacher." She winked at him and the two shared a brief silent exchange.

The rest of the band looked at Danius eagerly awaiting his explanation of why science is fun.

Danius shifted uncomfortably in his seat. "Well, there's an element of science in everything. I think that's why I like it so much. I mean the very word *science* means the observation and experimental investigation of natural phenomena like um…Pearl's singing voice, for instance. There's a scientific reason as to why she sings so beautifully that goes beyond just practice."

Pearl giggled and nudged him with her elbow. "Stop it."

"Is there a scientific reason Pearl blushed just now?" asked Emily.

"I did not blush." Pearl argued. "Look at me. Is this the complexion of a woman who blushes?"

"Did your face feel hot?" asked Patrick.

"A little."

"You blushed."

"Well, professor?" asked Emily.

Danius smiled self-consciously. "Well, blushing is more psychological than scientific but um…it has to do with the blood vessels in our faces. They dilate which causes an increase in blood flow to the area. And the blood vessels in our cheeks are wider and closer to the surface. And uh…well, there's this whole thing about the emotion associated with self-consciousness, which releases adrenaline, which causes the blood vessels to dilate and so on. It's involuntary too. So you can't control it and everyone does it no matter how light or dark their skin is."

"Wow! You really are more than just a pretty face." said Emily.

"And look at those blood vessels dilating." Lewis remarked about Danius's blush.

"Meanwhile my face is still hot. Let's talk about another natural occurrence." said Pearl.

"Yeah, like what's going on inside your brother's stomach?" asked Michael. "He's plowing through the 'Stuff' like a tractor.

"All day." Josiah reiterated.

"No. I got one." said Cary. "Ocean liners float, but rocks sink. What's up with that?"

"Ooh, I know that one!" said Emily. "It's because of the air inside the ship, right?"

Danius smiled. "That's right. The air inside of an object and even its shape can help it float on water. It's because of something called displacement. Displacement means to move something from one place to another and this Greek guy named Archimedes discovered that the amount of water displaced by an object depends on the mass of that object. That's why a cruise ship can weigh a thousand tons and still float because it displaces a thousand tons of water-and the rule is, an object will float if it weighs less than the water it displaces-then the pressure from below pushes up on the ship and causes it to float. Conversely a rock will sink because it's solid all the way through, no air. And because of its shape it doesn't displace the water around it. A good experiment to try would be to drop a spoon in dish water and, of course, it's going to sink. But put that same spoon inside of a bowl and put the bowl on the water and see what happens. It floats."

"Wow" was the only word that came to mind. Pearl sat in awe at the brilliant mind of Danius Todd. With every scientific question the guys threw at him, he came even more alive. Why was he writing instructions for computer programs and house-hold cleansers and diaper cream when he so obviously had a passion for teaching? It stood out all over him. His eyes sparkled. He smiled and his voice didn't have that faint note of annoyance in it. Why, it looked as if Mr. Todd was actually enjoying himself. Pearl just rested her cheek in her palm and her elbow on the table and listened. Wow!

Wow! Danius couldn't believe these people were actually interested in this stuff. Usually when he expounded too long on any subject Alexandria's eyes would glaze over. And here was Pearl, sitting next to him, resting her chin in her hand and hanging on to his every word. Was it a game? He wondered. Were they all just humoring him? He couldn't be sure but judging by the looks on all their faces-even Josiah was listening as he chewed-they certainly looked interested.

"You know who you remind me of?" Pearl asked Danius. "Mr. Wizard. You guys remember that show? It used to come on Nickelodeon."

"Oh, yeah." said Patrick. "He would have these kids doing science experiments with house-hold stuff."

Just as they were revisiting children's programs from the late 80s and 90s a tall, gangly, long-haired teenage boy stood directly in front of their table and performed a looping trick with his yo-yo by launching the yo-yo down the center of their table and looping it into a sleeping, pendulum. And just as quick as he appeared, he disappeared leaving Danius, Pearl and the rest of the band speechless. That is until Michael broke the silence.

Looking at Danius he said, "Yo-yos. Go."

To which Danius smiled and answered, "It's a combination of Potential energy when you hold the yo-yo in your hand and Kinetic energy when you let it go."

Everyone including Josiah laughed. Michael high-fived him and suddenly Danius didn't care if they were humoring him or not. He liked these people, especially the person sitting next to him.

She looked at him with her warm, brown eyes, shook her head and said, "You genius you."

He'd been fighting the urge to look at her, but he figured two seconds couldn't hurt anything. It turned out to be two seconds too long. For in that time his brain released a concoction of dopamine, norepinephrine and serotonin; sort of like a hormonal smoothie. But for all the lay people out there who couldn't give a hoot about science, it simply meant he was dangerously attracted to Pearl. And it had to stop.

How do you pronounce *Iaomai*?

After piling up into the van later that night, Josiah was twenty-five dollars richer but needed a ginger-ale for his stomach and Emily announced she was in dire need of hot tea with honey. So they stopped at a convenience store right outside of a town called Jupiter.

Danius hadn't packed anything so he needed toiletry items. Josiah ran away from home without deodorant, which he definitely needed. Lewis had to go to the restroom and Pearl had a sweet tooth. The rest of the guys stayed in the van.

They browsed around a bit in the fairly large mini-mart. Since it was right off the interstate, the store had plenty of travel goodies. Pearl hit the mother-load when she got to the candy aisle. She was going for the dark chocolate M&Ms when she heard Emily and Josiah chatting nearby.

"So what's this Alexandria person like?" Emily asked in a whisper loud enough for Pearl to hear.

Josiah scoffed and didn't even try to whisper, "She's pretty and annoying. She's pretty annoying."

Emily laughed and so did Pearl as she continued to eavesdrop.

"I'm serious." Josiah said. "She thinks the whole world revolves around her. She's stuck-up and bossy and treats Danius like he's her personal slave. I mean, she's so bad, my parents can't even stand her and they like *everybody*."

"Your brother's a smart guy. Why is he still with her?"

"He's book smart mostly. I mean, he's smart in other ways, too, just not when it comes to girls. That's why I'm kind of glad we're here. I think he should be with Pearl. I'd definitely ask her out if I was her age…or if she were my age. How old is Pearl, anyway?"

Pearl thought it would be a good time to interrupt the conversation. She rounded the Little Debbie snacks and met them in front of the coffee kiosk. "Hey, guys. Wow, Earl Grey! You know, for a convenience store in the middle of nowhere, they certainly have a large assortment of fine teas. Josiah, I would like to talk girl to girl with Emily if I may."

"You want me to leave you alone?"

"Yes I do."

"What's the magic word?"

Pearl gave Emily a smirk then turned back to Josiah. "Tampons."

"Ugh!" Grossed out, Josiah left immediately.

"No one can clear a room like you can." said Emily.

"It's a gift. Now do you want to tell me what you were doing asking that kid about his brother's girlfriend?"

"Just doing a little investigative research on your behalf; you know, a little reconnaissance. You're welcome, by the way."

"Thank you, Captain Cho, but you better abort the mission.

"Why?"

"Look, all we're doing is helping the guy out, not trying to ruin his life."

"Maybe his life should be ruined…for the better, I mean. He's kind of a square."

"He's a nice square." Pearl smiled as she took a glimpse of Danius at the other end of the store.

"Hmm. Are you sure you don't want me to do a little digging? Because you seem a tad interested."

"Even if I was, he's not. So there you have it."

"Okay, maybe you didn't see the way he was looking at you, but I did. I know I'm not the *smartest* knife in the drawer but I can tell when guy 'like' likes a girl."

" 'Like' likes? What, are we in the 8th grade? Can I borrow your notes for English class?"

They laughed.

"Okay." Emily acquiesced. "I'll leave it alone for now. But as my grandmother used to say…"

Whatever Emily's grandmother used to say was lost on Pearl because Emily recited it in Korean.

"Did your grandmother know any English sayings? Because I have no idea what you just said."

"Neither do I and I can translate it. But I know she said it all the time." Emily made her way to the check-out counter and paid for her tea.

Pearl could only smile at her well-meaning, yet misguided friend. Sure she'd noticed Danius on several occasions looking at her with that spark of attraction in his eyes but what could she do? The man had a girlfriend. She shook her head and continued browsing.

"Hey Danius and Josiah, they got t-shirts back here." Pearl announced from the back of the store near the restrooms. The brothers followed her voice.

"T-shirts?" Danius asked.

"Well, yeah. You don't strike me as a man who likes to marinate in the same clothes two days in a row." Turning to Josiah she said, "And you. The next time you run away from home, pack some deodorant and a clean shirt. Travel has made you a little ripe, homie."

Josiah took one whiff of his arm pit and had to agree. "I'll remember that next time."

"Now, had you run away with the circus, they would've kicked you out by now. They don't put up with bad hygiene."

The three of them bantered like that for about a minute with Pearl insisting Danius let her pay for the shirts because she knew he hadn't brought enough money with him. Then the bell above the door jingled and suddenly they heard a scream and someone yelling, "Everybody get down on the floor!"

Instinctively, Danius and Pearl both grabbed Josiah and pulled him down with them. They were on the last aisle closest to the restrooms. Pearl looked up at the reflection in the glass door of the refrigerator that held the sodas. She could see Emily and Lewis on the floor along with two other customers and a hand that held a gun right above them.

"You know what I want, fat boy. Put the money in the bag now!" The deep voice demanded.

Pearl, Danius and Josiah remained as quiet as they could even to the point of holding their breath. Hopefully the robber wouldn't look in the over-head security mirror and spot them on the floor. While the robber shouted orders for everyone to give up any jewelry they had and for the cashier to hurry up with the money, Pearl looked at Danius and mouthed, "We have to do something."

Danius held his hands out and shrugged as if to say, "What?"

She motioned him to give her his iPhone. Danius pulled it out of its case and glanced at it and produced a shocked expression on his face. When Pearl asked what, he pointed to the screen which read, "9 missed calls." Pearl made a face at him and snatched the phone. Thank God she had the presence of mind to make sure the phone's ringer was turned off. She texted Patrick, who was still in the van, *"Call 911. Store being robbed."*

That was all Pearl had planned to do, but then the situation escalated when she heard the cashier say he couldn't open the safe because only the manager of the store knew the combination. She looked at the glass and saw the gunman point the gun at the head of a female customer who began to hyperventilate from panic.

"Shut up!" he screamed.

"Oh, God, please help us?" Pearl prayed nearly out loud. Then an idea dropped into her mind and peace steadied her heart. She pulled off her flip-flop sandals and motioned for Danius and Josiah to follow her. Slowly and very quietly, they crawled away from the round mirror and closer to the slushy machine. The machine had an on-going drone so hopefully the noise would cover their whispering.

There, Pearl explained the plan. Not surprisingly, Danius disagreed with it, but who knew how long it would take the cops to get there? It had already felt like forever since she'd texted Patrick.

"Don't mess with me, man. You better *find* a way to open that safe!" The gunman shouted expletive after expletive when the cashier adamantly swore he could not open the safe. They heard Lewis offering up his vintage, gold pocket watch that was worth a lot of money. The situation was getting worse by the second. Pearl looked at Danius, pleading with her eyes, until he finally nodded his agreement to cooperate with the plan.

Getting into position was probably the most pain-staking part of the whole thing because it had to be done quietly. Danius crawled down the aisle. His part in this scheme would be to surprise the robber and hopefully immobilize him long enough for the others to do their part. When he looked on the shelves on either side of him an idea like lightning flashed in his mind. He would make his own version of pepper-spray.

On his left were empty spray bottles. On his right, on the middle shelf there were bottles of hot-sauce. On the bottom shelf there were bottles of vinegar. Danius turned to look at Pearl and Josiah and held up his index finger, motioning her to wait just one minute.

It was the longest minute of his life but quietly and very carefully he managed to pour the hot sauce and the vinegar into a spray bottle, always keeping an eye on the over-head mirror.

The robber continued to demand money and valuables. Danius thought his heart was going to leap right out of his chest, it was beating so fast. He turned and gave Pearl a thumb's up and they each got into place.

When all three were in place, the execution of Pearl's plan happened quickly and seamlessly. Pearl played the police siren ring tone on Danius's phone as loud as it could go. The gunman turned and looked out the door. Then Josiah created another diversion by knocking over cans of soup. The robber pointed the gun in the direction of the noise and pulled the trigger, blowing a hole in the slushy machine; pink and yellow slushy was all over the floor.

With all the screaming going on, Danius, one aisle away, whispered a prayer and made his way around the aisle. Standing directly behind the gunman, he yelled, "Hey!" When the bandit turned around Danius got him right in the eyes with the pepper-spray. The robber yelled out in pain, covering his eyes. Then Danius picked up the heaviest thing he could find-a bottle of bleach-and hurled it as hard as he could at the gunman's head, knocking him off his feet.

When the robber was down, Lewis-kicking his gun away-and another male customer kept him pinned until Pearl and Josiah could tie his hands and feet together, rodeo style, with the extension cords that were on sale. Then it was over; just like that and just in time for the police to take over.

They all watched as young Elijah Ohanzee was placed in the back of the police cruiser and taken away. "Elijah." Pearl mused. *The Lord is my God. May he make that true in his life."

It was nearly one in the morning when all was said and done. Now they stood in front of the store talking. The couple who had been in the store crouched down next to Emily and Lewis approached Pearl and Danius, introduced themselves as John and Amanda Nicholas and handed them their card. "We just wanted to thank you for what you did." said Amanda. "You all are real life heroes."

Then John added, "We owe you our lives. Listen, here's our card. Please let us know if there's anything we can do for you. All of you."

Pearl took their card. The Nicholases were doctors on a medical ship called *Iaomai*. One by one the members of the band tried to pronounce the word as they passed the card back and forth. Danius just listened. He heard everything from "EE ow may" to "Yo mah" to "Yao Ming," Michael's contribution.

John Nicholas chuckled and corrected them. "Ee-ah-om-ahee" He pronounced. "It's a greek word that means 'to heal' or 'to make whole.'

All together the band repeated the word correctly like a group of kindergartners. "Ee-ah-om-ahee."

"That's right." said the doctor. "See, we sail all year long to different countries and provide medical attention for people who either don't have a hospital in their town or can't afford to go to a hospital. We also share the Gospel with them. We stop over in the states to restock our supplies and visit our folks. We'll be heading out day after tomorrow, or at least that's what we're supposed to do. I don't know. With what happened tonight, maybe our plans have changed.

That last statement struck a chord with Danius. His plans and routined lifestyle had changed two days ago. As a matter of fact, it was right after meeting Pearl. He wasn't used to letting things just happen. He felt so helpless and lost. The Nicholases, however, though visibly upset about being held up at gun point, didn't seem to mind being "detoured," so to speak.

"Well, whatever happens," Amanda Nicholas said "God is in control."

"Just like he was tonight." said John.

"And I can't thank you enough for what you did." She continued.

Pearl took Amanda's hand and gave it a squeeze. "To be honest, I was scared out of my mind. But like you said, God was in control. I was wondering if we could all pray before you go."

"Oh, of course!" said John.

They formed a circle, took one another's hand and offered up praise and thanksgiving to God for his protection, his peace and his salvation, not just for them but for Elijah Ohanzee and the cashier who turned in his resignation that night.

Patrick declared he was too keyed up to sleep and opted to do the driving back up the coast. He got no argument. They all decided it would be pointless to check into a motel once they got to their next town. It was almost a three hour drive from Jupiter and once they got there, they would be performing in another seven hours, so they agreed to finding a rest stop and catching a few hours of sleep in the van.

On the road, Michael kept Patrick company in the front while the others picked their spots and dozed. Josiah slept with his head on Danius's lap, something he hadn't done since he was a toddler. It made Danius feel awkward and yet protective of his brother for the first time ever. And that protective feeling extended to the young woman sitting by the window on the passenger side. She was staring out at the pitch black scenery as he stared at her and wished for the hundredth time that night that he had been braver.

Once the Nicholases left and the adrenaline had worn off, Pearl had broken down, shaking and in tears. She'd covered her face with her hands and sobbed. Even then Danius hadn't been brave enough to hold her. It had been Patrick that rushed to comfort her while Danius looked on experiencing a rare feeling of jealousy.

"You should call her and let her know you're all right." Pearl said to him just then. He'd been caught staring at her.

"Who?" He asked when he recovered.

"Ms. Nine-missed-calls."

Alexandria. "Oh…well…It's after three in the morning…I…I couldn't call her now."

"You've been missing all day long. If she loves you, she won't care what time it is. She just wants to hear your voice. I mean, if I were in love with somebody, I think that's how I would feel."

Danius only nodded. "Are you…all right? I'm sorry I didn't…I couldn't…"

"I'm all right."

"But you were crying before."

"Relieving tension, I guess. Believe me, I would've cried in the store if we'd had time."

"But you didn't. You were so…brave. I wasn't."

"You sprayed an armed robber in the eyes with a bottle of pepper-spray that you *made* in under a minute. That's not only brave, that's…MacGyver."

Danius smiled and Pearl smiled right back at him.

"I just can't help but think if I would've just-

"Danius don't. Please don't do that to yourself. The what-ifs and if-onlys will drive you crazy. God was with us tonight as he always is. Just thank him."

With that, Pearl turned her focus back on the dark scenery. Danius turned to his window and did the same. He closed his eyes, took in a deep breath and breathed out a sincere "Thank you."

He hadn't known he was asleep until the squeal of the van brakes woke him up. The dome light overhead only lit so much, but he could tell that except for Patrick, everyone else including Michael had dropped off to sleep. He watched Patrick rub his eyes and shake his head several times while waiting for the light to turn green. Danius didn't know where they were or how much farther they had to go but he decided to help Patrick stay alert.

"Where are we?" He asked in soft tones.

"Right outside Daytona." Patrick answered in equally soft tones.

"Are you okay? I could drive for you if you want."

"That's all right. The rest stop is up ahead about a mile. So…it's been quite a night, huh? How are you doing after all that?"

"I guess I'm all right, but I can't get the image of that guy's face out of my head. The look in his eyes…if it hadn't gone down the way that it did, he would've killed somebody for sure. We were lucky."

Patrick drove on. "I don't think I'd call it luck. You have no idea how hard Cary, Michael and I were praying here until the police came. When the gun went off…" He shook his head. "If Michael hadn't pinned me down, I would've come charging through those doors, completely unarmed, and who knows? We might not be having this conversation now."

"Then I guess I wouldn't call it luck either."

Patrick turned into the rest stop and parked. Both he and the van seemed to sigh when he shut off the ignition.

"I should be more like Michael. "Patrick said. "He's always cool under pressure."

"It must run in the family." said Danius as he turned to look at Pearl sleeping peacefully on the other side of Josiah.

Patrick turned to look too. Danius couldn't see his face, it was a silhouette against the glow of the street light, but he could hear his deep sigh. Once again Danius felt a jolt of jealousy. Why should he be jealous though? It made absolutely no sense. Pearl wasn't his, so why should he feel so possessive of her? But he did and it prompted him to ask, "You…care about her a lot, don't you?"

"Of course I do. She's very special to me."

Danius didn't know how to respond to that one so he remained silent while his chest tightened.

"You know she's the one who introduced me to my fiancé." said Patrick.

Fiance?

"I don't think I could love Pearl more if she were my own sister." With that Patrick reclined his seat, crossed his arms over his chest and drifted off to sleep in less than three minutes.

Danius began to breathe easier, aware that he had been holding his breath. Patrick was engaged to be married to someone else and Danius was relieved. But he shook his head, absolutely disgusted with himself, because of this irrational attraction to Pearl.

"What's wrong with me?" He actually said out loud.

"You have a girlfriend but you like Pearl and it's tearing you up inside." Patrick answered without opening his eyes or making a stir. "Now go back to sleep."

Danius stared out at the street light outside his window for a moment, then closed his eyes and pondered Patrick's very accurate summation.

Danius in Wonderland

He walked down a long, dusty road, checking the time on his iPhone every few seconds. "I have to get there on time. I can't be late." He said to no one in particular.

Get where? He wondered. At the moment he couldn't remember where he was supposed to be but he knew he had to be there soon.

Just then a blue Buick Regal pulled up next to him. The man driving it looked haggard, dirty and homeless but seemed nice enough. There was a young man in the back seat that Danius didn't particularly like although he couldn't quite put his finger on the reason why.

"Get in." said the driver. "You don't want to be late."

Danius didn't hesitate. He got in. Sitting in the front passenger seat, he turned to look at the man in the back who was busy counting money and checking his gold pocket watch. "Why don't I like you?" He asked out loud, surprising only himself.

The man shrugged but didn't speak. He just kept counting his money.

Danius turned around to face the front. He checked his iPhone again for the correct time. He had ten minutes to get there. Where?

"Remind me where I'm supposed to be again." he said to the driver.

"You're due in court in ten minutes. It's on your schedule. Didn't you check it?"

"Oh, court. That's right." Danius checked the calendar app on his phone. As he checked the agenda for each day, he became more and more confused. Every day said *Court in ten minutes.*

"I don't think you're gonna make it." said the man in the back seat. Only he didn't *say* it. He screamed it and scared Danius so much that he pepper-sprayed the man.

The young man covered his eyes and screamed in agony but a few minutes later he was again counting his money and looking at his watch.

Danius couldn't figure out where he got the pepper-spray from, but he was glad he had it. Every time the young man opened his mouth, Danius would spray him. The man would scream and then go back to counting money. This became routine as they rode along.

"When are we going to get to the courthouse?" Danius asked. And the next thing he knew the driver had driven them not only to the courthouse but up the stairs and right into the courtroom.

"It's about time!" screamed the man in the back.

Danius sprayed him again then exited the car.

It was just a run-of-the-mill courtroom with its varnished wood and shiny brass, except for the Buick parked in the middle of it.

"Counselor, how does your client plead?" asked the judge, looking directly at Danius.

The first thing Danius noticed was the judge, who looked exactly like Alexandria. The second thing he noticed was that he was grossly unprepared and not only that. He had no idea what a lawyer was supposed to do. Standing at the defense table he glanced over at his client; a boy, who looked just liked Josiah, dressed as a court jester with his face painted as a mime. Danius examined the jester's attire up and down. Who wears a jester's costume to court?

"Why are you dressed like that?" he asked.

The jester did not speak. He only made a sweeping arch with his hand to indicate they were in a *court*room and then smoothed down the front of his yellow and red costume, the bells on his three-pointed, cloth hat jingling with the motion.

"This is a different kind of court." Danius whispered. "What are you here for, anyway?"

The jester shrugged his shoulders.

"Mr. Todd?" said the judge. "I have a full calendar this morning. I'd like to have your client's plea today, as this is his first appearance in court."

"Uh…yes, sir…ma'am. Your Honor. Please, may I have a moment?"

The jester tapped Danius on the arm and motioned him to lean down so he could whisper to him.

"You know, you're not saying anything. You're just moving your lips." Danius said matter-of-factly.

The jester lifted his hand and pointed with his chin toward the judge, giving Danius the go-ahead to enter his plea.

Her Honor impatiently tapped her manicured nails on the bench. "Are you ready, Mr. Todd?"

Danius nervously fidgeted with his tie. "Uh…Your Honor, I really don't know what my client did—is *accused* of doing, I mean. I don't know why he's here. I don't know why I'm here.

"Mr. Todd, your client is accused of escaping a maximum security mime detention facility. As you, no doubt, are aware, the practice of mimetry has been outlawed for some time now."

"Uh…I think the word is *mimicry…or miming.*"

"Do you presume to correct me in my own courtroom, Mr. Todd?"

"No ma'am."

"Very well. As I was saying, all juvenile mimes are to be henceforth retained in a secured, state facility until their eighteenth birthdays. After which, they are to spend the remainder of their lives on the Lamu Island off the coast of Africa. To escape from said secured facility is a federal offence and the fact that your client is here and not there does not bode well with the court. But even a mime has the right to a fair trial and you as his lawyer are appointed to represent him in this matter."

Danius rubbed his fingers across his forehead, trying to comprehend what the judge had said. He had the feeling of someone, who couldn't swim, being pushed into a pool. In his panic he cried out, "I don't want to be a lawyer!"

Unfazed, the judge said, "Nevertheless you are one and you'll do your job or be held in contempt. Now how does he plead?"

Danius looked at his client and repeated, "How do you plead?"

The jester walked around to the front of the defense table, got down on his knees and clasped his hands together in front of him in a begging gesture.

"Mr. Todd!"

"I don't know…uh…guilty?"

"Very well. This case will be passed for sentencing one month from today. Counselor, call the next case."

The jester gave Danius a dirty look then stood and put his wrists together in front of him, mimicking a person turning himself in. Two bailiffs who looked an awful lot like Cary and Lewis came and escorted the jester to a holding cell.

"Next case, Mr. Todd." said the judge.

Danius looked around the courtroom for any sort of clue. Not finding any, he looked pleadingly to the judge. "Please, Your Honor. I don't know what the next case is. I don't know what I'm doing."

"Mr. Todd, your ineptedness astounds me."

"*Ineptitude*." he corrected.

"Counselor, you're out of order!" yelled the judge.

The man who'd been in the back seat of the Buick was suddenly standing next to Danius. He laughed and Danius sprayed him in the eyes.

Then everyone started to laugh: the judge, the clerk, the court reporter who looked like Emily, the bailiffs, the private attorneys-Michael and Patrick look-alikes-and the spectators; everyone except the young woman in the back of the courtroom.

She was wearing a cream colored sun-dress that seemed to dance in the wind. But there was no wind in the courtroom. Her auburn-tipped dreadlocks framed her face and her smile nearly hid her eyes. She was beautiful.

Danius felt inexplicable warmth pour over him at the sight of her. He took a step in her direction but the sound of a banging gavel stopped him in his tracks. He looked back at the judge.

"Mr. Todd, you haven't been excused from my courtroom yet." said the judge.

"I need to talk to her, Judge." He explained.

"You take one step in the wrong direction and you will regret it."

There Danius stood in the middle of the courtroom looking back and forth from the beautiful woman in the back to the judge in the front, torn between his duty and his desire. Which way was the wrong direction? "God, I don't know what to do." he said out loud.

Back Seat Guy laughed and loudly proclaimed in front of everybody, "You're a punk, man!"

That was the final straw. Danius emptied out his can of pepper-spray in the face of this man then shoved him in the back seat of the Buick. Then one by one he grabbed everybody, including the judge and shoved them all into the car as well; everyone that is except for the young lady at the back of the courtroom.

Not the least bit surprised that they all fit in the car, Danius bent down to look at the driver. "Just drive. Drive as far away from here as you can."

The world-weary driver didn't respond, he just put the car in 'drive' and drove forward out of sight.

Danius and the young lady were alone now. He felt peace wash over him as he walked toward her. When they were standing face to face, Danius slipped his arms around her waist as she slipped her arms around his neck.

"I should've held you." he said. He noticed they were now standing in the middle of a beautiful garden with birds chirping, wind blowing through the trees and soft music coming from an unknown source. He looked deep into her chocolate-brown eyes and could swear he saw images of laughing children projected in them. It made him smile. He lightly caressed her cheek. "Oh, Pearl." he whispered.

She smiled up at him. He lowered his mouth to hers…

The Return of the Blue Buick

When he opened his eyes, light poured in through the windows. He was met with three different sounds; snoring from just about everybody in the van, bird sounds, including a woodpecker who didn't care if there were humans trying to sleep, and a lone guitar playing so soft and sweet it almost lulled him back to dream land. He climbed over his brother's sprawled form on the bench seat and looked out the window. They were now in the parking lot of a Wal-Mart and right outside the van sat Pearl, reclined, in a plastic beach chair with an opened Bible at her bare feet. She was playing notes on her guitar. Danius just watched. Periodically she would flip a page and read, then lay back again, close her eyes and continue playing. She was so beautiful.

But the sight of her communing with God unsettled Danius. So he turned away.

"I miss you." The Voice said.

"Where have I been?" Danius almost asked out loud. He shook his head. He didn't really want to know the answer to that. But all at once he began to recognize how far he had distanced himself from the faith he once knew.

He remembered what the Bible said about faith being the substance of things hoped for and the evidence of things not seen. It was the "things not seen" that Danius had a problem with.

Before Josaiah was born and before his parents knew Christ, Danius's childhood was full of uncertainty. From one day to the next he didn't know if he would eat or have a place to sleep. He was born to teenage parents who were madly in love but had no clue about responsibility or priorities; about what it meant to put their own needs aside for the sake of their child.

Having no sense of purpose, Gary Todd would lose a job as quickly as he could get one, always finding fault with an employer or the procedures they practiced. Gloria Todd would pick up the slack with her two jobs, but that left Danius to practically raise himself.

There were times when Gloria felt entitled to use her hard earned money her way even if it meant neglecting a few of the bills. Danius remembered at least three separate occasions where they had to leave their home and stay with relatives for a while, sleeping on couches, floors and even sharing one bed. There were times when Danius was sent by himself to live with relatives and didn't see his parents for days.

Then somehow the bills would get squared away, Gary would find another job and Gloria would come and get her son. For a while there would be peace in their home and then the whole cycle would start all over again.

All of this made Danius a very nervous boy. He would lay awake at night wondering if this would be the night his father would come home and announce his boss was an idiot and he wasn't going back to work for an idiot. Both dreading and expecting the announcement, Danius kept a notebook at the ready filled with the names and numbers of all the family members who lived in the state. He began keeping track of the bills and what days they were due. Gloria thought it was sweet, he was Mama's helper. But Danius was old enough to know the smoother the transition from apartment to relatives' spare-room when Dad lost his job the less his parents would argue.

Danius couldn't control everything but he could keep his grades up and the apartment cleaned so it would be one less thing for his parents to fight over. In order to keep track of all he had to do, Danius made a schedule for himself and stuck to it. Before long and without his parent's noticing, he was running his own life like a well-oiled machine. He liked that feeling of control he had over his own life.

Then the inevitable happened. Dad had quit one of the best paying jobs he'd ever had, citing his employer and coworkers with incompetence. Mom got down right belligerent and said she was sick and tired of his foolishness while Danius sat stoically in the corner and made a list of things that needed to be done before they were evicted.

But in a strange turn of events, Gloria Todd announced she'd had enough, packed a duffel bag and left their apartment, leaving Danius and his father stunned and speechless. That wasn't supposed to happen. Danius thought. It upset the whole routine that he was used to; one that he had worked out on paper.

He grabbed his notebook and pen and was poised to write, but broke down in tears instead. Gary didn't speak. He just sat there rubbing Danius's back.

As it turned out, that was the start of a complete overhauling of the Todd family. Gloria was gone nearly a month and in that time she'd begun to attend church with some friends. She invited Gary and Danius one Sunday and as a family all three went down to the altar and received Christ as their savior. Danius was nine years old.

Things changed for the better. Gary and Gloria embraced their new faith and never looked back. Gary fell in love with carpentry and started his own business. Gloria became a claims adjuster for an insurance company and was able to work from home. Within two years they were living in their own house and Danius couldn't have been happier. But he continued to keep a watchful eye, waiting for the bottom to fall out. It never did. Still he couldn't shake the need to have some control over his destiny, believing in God but never fully relying on him to have everything under control.

So Danius became a micro manager of every aspect of his life. It was better that way. He thought. He'd be one less person God had to worry about; works out for everybody, right? Then why did that Voice rock him to his core with the words, "I miss you?" And why was Danius about two seconds away from admitting the same?

Suddenly the van seemed to grow smaller. He quietly made his way outside and took several deep breaths.
"Good morning." said Pearl.
Danius placed a hand on his chest and cleared his throat. "Good morning." he said raspingly.
"You okay?"
His first inkling was to say I don't know but instead he said, "Yeah. I just needed to stretch my legs. Sorry for interrupting your studying."
Pearl moved her legs and sat up straight to make room for him. "That's okay. Grab some beach chair and join me." She patted the empty spot with her hand.
Danius opened his mouth to decline but decided to join her. Anything was better than being left alone with his thoughts. "Is this your early morning routine?"
"Yeah. I try to get alone with God for a little while each day but, to tell you the truth, I'm not a real morning person. I know it's hard to believe, right? But it's hard to sleep sitting up and even harder to sleep when you have a twelve-year-old boy's foot imbedded in your side."
Danius laughed and stretched to awaken his muscles.
"And then there's just something about thwarting a robbery that just keeps the mind busy." she said rather seriously.
Danius looked at Pearl with understanding in his eyes and nodded his head. "Yeah." was all he could say.
They were silent for a while until Danius asked, "What book are you in?" referring to her Bible.

"Oh, Proverbs. I read this the other day and it stuck with me. Chapter 16 verse 9; A man's heart devises his way: but the Lord directs his steps. How's that for GPS?"

"Frightening."

"Yeah, but comforting too. At least I think so."

"I wish I could be more like you, just blindly following the Lord with no fear."

"Whoever said I was fearless? I was very scared last night. And in life, I'm supposed to be *sober* and *vigilant*, you know, watching out for my adversary, the devil. Does that sound like blindly following Jesus to you?"

"No I guess not."

It was as if Pearl could look past his eyes and see the questions and the doubt in his mind. With her closed Bible she tapped him on his knee. "Hey, it's not all that hard. God is like GPS. Follow his directions and he'll get you where you need to go."

She made it sound so easy. Why then did it seem so hard for Danius?

Wal-Mart proved to be the perfect rest stop. They all ate breakfast at the in-store McDonald's and washed up as best they could in the restrooms. Thanks to Pearl, Danius and Josiah had deodorant, toothbrushes, toothpaste and new shirts, but Danius drew the line at letting her pay for the underwear. By the time they made it back to the van it was time to head on over to the nursing home for their first gig of the day.

Danius was again amazed by the band's professionalism and skill and their ability to relate to their audience. This time they played classic Jazz and swing music from the 30s and 40s. Their audience, mostly octogenarians, sang along, pleased and very impressed by the young musicians. The best part came near the end when Pearl and Emily recreated a Judy Garland/Barbra Streisand duet; a medley starting with a song called, *Hooray for Love*.

For this they moved off the stage and into the audience. Thoroughly entertaining, they even stopped the music to do a comedy routine where they argued over who got to hit Judy Garland's show-stopping, high note. The program director was so impressed she begged the band to come back…and soon.

The next stop was a half-way house for young women. Here, Pearl talked to the girls about her childhood and how she, her brother and sister had been abused and neglected, left to fend for themselves for days at a time until their aunt and uncle found them, took them into their home and raised them.

She had Danius's undivided attention for the next thirty minutes as she talked candidly about her determination to be as unlike her mother as she could possibly be; making straight A's in school, avoiding men like the plague, working her way through college and then working her way up the corporate ladder. She was so focused, with such a one-track mind about succeeding, that she alienated family and friends and stressed herself out to the point of collapse.

An illness that the doctors could not diagnose nearly took her life. And it was in a dark hospital room, hooked up to machines that kept her awake with all their bells and whistles that she heard God's voice, still and small, but could be heard over all the noise. "As clearly as I'm talking to you," she said. "I heard the voice of the Lord say, '*You're killing yourself trying to prove you're not your mother, but you don't have to. I know who you are. I made you. I know who I created you to be. If you allow me to be your Savior and Lord and follow me, you will grow into that person.*"

Pearl began to play softly on her keyboard while she spoke and continued to encourage the young women. "You know something? The same is true for you. There's a scripture in the Bible, the book of Jeremiah, chapter 29 verse 11 which says, *'For surely I know the plans I have for you, says the Lord, plans for your welfare and not for harm, to give you a future with hope.'* Then it goes on to say, *'Then when you call upon me and come and pray to me, I will hear you. When you search for me, you will find me; if you seek me with all your heart, I will let you find me, says the Lord...'*

'Oh, girls, God loves you so much. He knows what you've done and what you've been through and he loves you still. Won't you seek him? It's like when I play hide and seek with my nephew. He always gives himself away by saying, 'Auntie! Come find me.' I believe that's how God is. If you seek him, he will *let* you find him. He let me find him that night in the hospital. A few days later I wrote this song and I want to sing it for you right now."

Pearl transitioned easily into the song and the band followed her lead. Danius was nearly moved to tears by her story as were a lot of the women in the audience. Pearl sang a soft, simple song about a sinner who asks for forgiveness.

Oh Lord of Lords
I can't run anymore
Now that I hear your voice
My heart is yours

Oh King of Kings
You are everything
That you said you'd be
Now I believe

Jesus, Jesus, Jesus

Come and save, Come to stay
I give my life to you today
You are the Son of God
Jesus, you are the way
And I believe
So come and save

I can't deny
Or justify
The way I've lived my life
I'm dead inside
And I'm ashamed
I know I'm to blame
And yet I hear you say to call your name

Jesus, Jesus, Jesus

Come and save, Come to stay
I give my life to you today
You are the Son of God
Jesus, you are the way
And I believe
So come and save

I'm a sinner
I've done you wrong
Will you forgive me for what I've done?
Make me clean
Make me your own
And I will live for
You alone

When it was over, some of the ladies asked her to help them pray and ask for the same.

Before the concert was over, the atmosphere had changed from one of repentance to celebration. So much so, that the ladies were up on their feet waving and clapping their hands, dancing and singing and just flat out having fun. That's when Danius realized that *Patiently Waiting* was not just a dime-a-dozen rock band, they were ministers and Pearl was not just a singer, she was a servant of God who was passionate about leading people to Christ and seeing their lives changed as her life had been.

Danius had grown quiet by the time they all got back on the road, as he was trying to digest everything he'd seen and heard today. "Plans." The last few days seemed to be about nothing but plans. He'd made plans. His plans got changed. Things happened that he hadn't planned on and now he had no plans. He was confused now. He wished the band would hurry and take him home so he could get back to his regularly scheduled life. It was comfortable, if not constant. And yet, he wished this crazy tour could go on forever. He wished somehow, he and Pearl could…

Saved by the bell. That line of thinking was interrupted by the ringing of his cell phone. It was Alexandria. *Oh, boy.*

He could barely get hello out before she ripped into him. "Well, where was your phone this time, Afghanistan?"

"No. West Palm Beach." He quickly answered.

"What?"

"Well…uh…there was an emergency and I had to drive down to West Palm Beach early yesterday morning."

"What emergency?"

"My brother. You see…he…we…it's a very long story. I intended to call you, but after the car got stolen…"

"Whose car?"

"My mother's. After that Josiah and I needed a ride back and the band was nice enough…"

"Wait a minute. What band?" She demanded.

"*Patiently Waiting*. They're very good, by the way."

"Danius, you're not making sense and you still haven't told me why you had to make an emergency trip to West Palm Beach."

The band chose that very moment to start singing along to a song on the radio; *I Got That Feelin'* by James Brown. The beep in his ear indicated that he had another call. His mother chose that very moment to call and check up on her sons.

"Uh…Alexandria could I call you right back?"

"Absolutely not! You stood me up yesterday and I demand an explanation."

"I'm trying to explain, but my mother's on the other line and I have to take this…just hold on, please, for a second."

"Danius, don't you put me on…"

He clicked over. "Hi, Mom!"

"Wow! That's the cheeriest hello I've gotten from you in a long time." Gloria said. "You and Joe havin' fun, huh?"

"Uh…yeah. Yes we are."

"Do I hear James Brown?"

"Yes you do. So Mom, how's the cruise going?"

"Oh, it's great! Did you know you can eat any time of the day or night on a cruise ship? I had lobster and a hot-fudge sundae at three o'clock this morning. Your daddy won the limbo contest an hour ago. I didn't know he was that flexible. He's been holding out on me. Oh, and the best part is you meet the most interesting people from all over the world. I met this Asian couple. They don't speak a word of English, but we're meeting them for dinner and a show. I'm not sure but I think Tito Jackson is performing."

The beep in his ear told him Alexandria was still holding on. "Mom, can you hold on? Alexandria's on the other line."

He clicked over only to find Alexandria still ranting. "...I called you nine times yesterday and do you mean to tell me you couldn't return *one* of my calls?"

Danius looked at the phone and shrugged, "I'm sorry, honey." He said.

"Don't honey me. You left me waiting at the museum for an hour and a half..."

Danius clicked over. "Mom?"

"I'm still here. Daddy just signed us up for karaoke so I have to go, but let me speak to Joe first."

Josiah was in the middle of *"Baby, baby, baaaby"* when Danius grabbed his shirt collar and pulled him toward the back of the camper.

"It's Mom." Danius whispered. "Okay, Mom, here's Josiah."

Josiah put the phone to his ear and held his mouth open but didn't speak. After almost a minute, he gave the phone back to Danius.

"She's doing all right." Josiah said. "They're about to sing *Ain't No Mountain High Enough* so she had to go. And who's Tito Jackson?"

"I'll tell you later." Danius said as he fumbled for the button on his phone.

James Brown was replaced by Al Green and Danius clicked over.

"...Well, what do you have to say for yourself?" Alexandria asked.

Danius scrambled for something appropriate to say "Uh...I'm really sorry. I can explain everything in detail, when I get home."

"When will that be?"

"I'm not sure."

"What about your meeting with Daddy?"

"What meeting with Daddy? Oh! The meeting, Oh, Alexandria I don't think I'll be able to make that meeting because I already had a meeting scheduled with Frederick Maxwell. He's designed a new software program and…"

"Danius, how you can continue to write silly instructions for people when Daddy is offering you a career in law is beyond me. You have a chance to work in his firm, to put yourself through law school and come back to work for him as an attorney in the most prestigious law firm in Jacksonville. He's practically handing you your future on a platter."

Just then Pearl made her way to the back of the van singing, *"…good or bad. Happy or sad."* She grabbed a bottle of water from the mini-fridge, shot Danius a wink and went back to her seat.

Danius stared after her, mesmerized with the words, "Your future" in his mind. He heard Alexandria ask, "Who was that singing?" in her exasperatingly, suspicious tone.

"Al Green." He said absentmindedly. "I have to go." This time he didn't wait for Alexandria's reply. He clicked off, stuck the phone back in his pocket and sighed heavily. He was right back where he started. Confused.

He's so cute when he's brooding, Pearl thought when she looked back at him. He was sitting alone in the back of the camper staring at the floor. When she'd met him a few days ago he'd been impeccably dressed in a suit and tie with not a hair out of place. Today, though, he wore his khaki pants with the t-shirt Pearl had bought him from Wal-Mart. He had two days' worth of stubble and his hair now sported the tiniest hint of a wave. Josiah was a miniature version of Danius and if his "brillo pad" head was any indication, Pearl figured that Danius would too have a mess of unruly curls if he allowed it to grow out.

But for all his good looks, he certainly looked sick right now. Pearl wished she knew what was on his mind. She wished she could help him somehow.

"You *can't help him with this.*" said the unmistakable voice of God.

Pearl closed her eyes and silently asked God what she could do.

"Pray. And be a friend."

But her feelings were a little more than friendly. "Easier said than done, God."

Still she had to try. The poor guy looked depressed as all get out.

Then she had an idea. She whispered to Emily who whispered to Michael who whispered to Patrick. Patrick turned the volume on the radio down and Michael began to make his own beat on the dashboard. Everyone joined in with their own sound effects.

Danius looked up and noticed everyone bobbing their heads to beats they were making themselves without the music. *What are these crazy people doing now?* He wondered. Whatever is was he wasn't in the mood for it. Then Pearl moved from the front of the camper to the back and sat next to him and surprised him with a rap.

Mr. Danius Todd
Why don't you flip that frown
Into a permanent position hanging upside down
On your face, we're gonna put a smile on it if you
want it
Admit it, rhymes in your honor make you want to
grin, don't it?
I know it wasn't you plan
To be stuck with a band

With her camera phone, Pearl snapped a picture of a surprised but smiling Danius. The rest of the band laughed and clapped and continued their free-styling with each person taking a turn coming up with a rap off the top of their head.

"There's that smile I've been looking for." said Pearl.

Danius looked down shyly. "Oh, Pearl I…" he looked into her warm brown eyes. He wanted so badly to talk to her about what was happening to him. He just couldn't. "Thank you." was all he could say.

"That's what I'm here for; to spread cheer." Pearl nudged him with her shoulder. She didn't know the scope of what all was bothering Danius. She had a pretty good idea though. It probably had something to do with what was bothering her. What to do? Of course they could let it slide since there was a chance they'd never see each other again after this weekend. But if they were going to be real friends, they were going to have to talk about their feelings for each other sooner or later.

While they were still in Daytona, Patrick suggested they go to one of the beach cafés since they had some time to kill. The Maxwell birthday party was going to be formal so it gave them a perfect excuse to shop. After lunch they covered the strip, weaving in and out of clothing stores until they each found the perfect evening attire, befitting a rock band, of course.

A peculiar sight to see was Lewis playing fight songs on the violin while the others played touch football on the beach. Even Danius had to get in on the game, especially after being hit with the ball several times because he wasn't paying attention.

At one point, Danius and Pearl fell over each other as they both tried to catch the ball. Sparks flew and Lewis accompanied them with the love theme from *Titanic*. He beautifully performed *We Are The Champions* for the winning team when the game was over as passersby cheered him on.

When Lewis' playing began to attract children and their parents, the other members of the band got their acoustic instruments and joined in, giving an impromptu performance.

Danius looked on and for a moment forgot about the last thirty or so hours; his runaway brother, his mother's car, the robbery, even Alexandria, and just enjoyed himself. For a moment his brain and his heart declared a cease-fire and he could breathe a little easier. How long this window of tranquility would stay open, Danius didn't know, but he was determined to milk every second of it.

As he watched Pearl singing and laughing with the kids who'd gathered around, he allowed the sound of the waves crashing, the warm sand under his feet, the cool breeze, the heat from the sun, the smell of the sea and the taste of salt in the air take him to a place where there were no problems. There was no future to worry about and no Alexandria to break his back trying to please.

What did he see in her anyway? He couldn't even remember, but it had something to do with his image. He'd been Danius the Dork from sixth grade on up into college. It was during his junior year at Jacksonville University that Alexandria sort of "took him on" as a project. She'd changed his hair, his clothes, his classes, even the friends he hung out with. He wasn't always comfortable with that, but it had seemed that spending time with J.U.'s "It" girl had boosted his popularity immensely. And he had liked it.

He fancied himself in love with Alexandria, so he would do things for her, buy her gifts, run her errands, take her to expensive restaurants that he couldn't afford. In return, she basically "let" him date her and as long as she was happy, he was happy being her little project or boyfriend or whatever he was.

Alexandria introduced Danius to the lifestyles of the moderately wealthy and locally well-known; to kids who worked just to bide time until their trust funds kicked in; to up-and-comers, who upon meeting Danius for the first time would always ask, "What are your plans for the future?" to which Danius would unashamedly reply, "I want to get my teaching degree and teach middle and high school students." That is until the day Alexandria interrupted and answered the question for him by saying, "I'm trying to convince Danius to go into law like Daddy. I keep telling him he's got such a wealth of knowledge on every subject imaginable, he should put it to *good* use such as: law and maybe politics."

The subtext in that comment told Danius that Alexandria did not approve of his life choices. Further subtext told him that if he wanted to be with her he had to do everything he could to make her happy, including give up his life-long dream.

He could feel his window of tranquility closing, so he walked down to where the water met his feet and took some deep breaths. A few minutes later Josiah joined him.

"Patrick told me if I stand here, the water will be up to my knees in an hour." Josiah said looking up at his brother.

"That's true."

"But how does he know that?"

"Well the high tide comes in twice a day, every day at certain times."

Josiah dug his toes into the sand. "Why?"

"Well, it has to do with the gravitational pull of the moon and Earth. You see, the gravitational attraction of the moon causes the oceans to bulge out in the direction of the moon."

Danius looked down at his brother and saw his furrowed brows. He wasn't getting it. Then he felt Pearl's presence before he saw her. He had no idea how he knew it was her, he just knew. She came and stood on the other side of Josiah.

"The Earth and the moon are attracted to each other." Pearl said. "Kind of like…" looking at Danius, "magnets to a refrigerator. And while the moon is pulling the Earth towards it, the Earth sort of pulls back, holding on to everything but the water. Is that right?" she asked Danius.

"Yeah, that's right." For a moment he was lost in her eyes then he remembered Josiah. "Wait a second." he said, then went over to a couple of kids building a sand-castle and asked to borrow their pale. He filled it with water and came back. "See Joe, it's like this. I'm the Earth and Pearl is the moon. This pale of water is the ocean. Pearl will hold on to one side of the pale and I'll hold on to the other. And as she pulls me toward her, the water is moving first in my direction then in her direction. See? And as I pull back, the water moves in her direction first then mine.

Now imagine the moon is circling me while I'm rotating and we're both circling you, the sun; all while still playing tug-o-war with the ocean. You see how the water is constantly moving?"

"Oh, I get it. Cool!" Josiah said as he grabbed the pale and shook the water back and forth. "I wish Mr. Rayburn taught us like this, maybe I wouldn't fall asleep in his class." Josiah poured the water out and gave the pale back to the kids.

Danius and Pearl noticed they were still standing very close to each other. Pearl took her attraction to him in stride, but Danius seemed visibly shaken most of the time and this time was no different. They were silent for an uncomfortable minute or so.

"Someone better say something before someone else sees us staring and says something stupid." said Pearl. "You like that alliteration?"

"Do you just come up with this stuff right off the top of your head?"

"Yes I do. It's a gift. Hey Danius, are you sure you want to be a lawyer? Because you're pretty good at this teaching thing."

He shrugged his shoulders and looked away trying to come up with an answer that would justify his decision. He came up empty. "What about you? You're an amazingly gifted singer and musician. Why don't you pursue that full time?"

"Because I like to eat and pay bills…and I worked on the business end of the music industry. I know what the stress and strain can do to a gifted singer or musician. It has a way of drawing the passion out of you until it becomes a chore and you no longer do it because you love it. You do it because you're bound by a contract. Or you do it to retain your popularity. And if I was stressed out from a business standpoint, I can only imagine how the artists felt.

"After my illness, I sat and asked God to help me figure out what to do with my life. I acquired the café from the man I use to work for in college: He was retiring. Then I started booking local musicians and singers. Just for fun, I would ask my friends from church to come in and play and that's how we got started. I'm not saying the music business as a whole is bad. I know I have the talent for it. I know I could be good at it. It's just not what I want to do with my life.

"I decided though that I would use every talent and gift that God has given me. I have a good head for business so I own and operate a café. I love to sing and play music so I joined a band. I love to draw and paint. Half of the art work in the café is mine and I even come up with logos for other businesses. I love talking to people about God and how he changed my life. And I absolutely love to write. I write some of the songs we sing and poetry and short stories. I guess you could call me a jack of all trades or something, I don't know. I just want whatever I do to point to the Savior. That's my dream."

"And you're certainly doing that." He looked away, staring at the distant horizon.

"What are you thinking about?"

What could he say to that? Pearl had invaded every inch of available space in his mind, but he couldn't very well *say* it was her he was thinking of.

Even though she was standing right next to him, he was wondering how she was doing. He wanted to know what she put in her hair to make it smell the way it did. He wanted to know how she got that scar underneath her eyebrow. It was faint and you had to be really looking at her to see it. He noticed her biting the inside of her bottom lip on several occasions. It was quirky and he wondered if she even knew she was doing it now. There were many other things about Pearl he wanted to know and all of these things ran through his mind, but he couldn't tell her that's what he was thinking. Somehow he thought he would be betraying Alexandria if he did.

"Just wondering about my window." he said. "I think it's closed."

Later on Danius decided to walk ahead of the others toward the van. He needed time to think, but all he could think about was Pearl. This was getting ridiculous. He'd fallen over her and for her all at once it seemed. When he'd helped her up during the football game and saw the look in her eyes he knew she felt it too. What a mess he was in. He had to get away from her, that's all. If he could just go somewhere by himself he could think rationally.

"Hey." Pearl said when she caught up to him. "You okay?"

"Yes…no…I don't know…Why wouldn't I be?" He snapped. "I just need to walk."

"I'll walk with you."

"No thanks."

"Why not?" she asked staying in step with him.

"I don't think it's such a good idea, Pearl."

"Why, 'cause you like me?"

He stopped in his tracks. "Like you?"

"You do, don't you?" She'd asked that the first time they met. It felt like a lifetime ago.

Danius paced back and forth in front of her. He was all set to deny her claim but what came out of his mouth was, "Yes! Yes I like you…a lot. More than I should. More than I care to mention. It bothers me. It makes me want to…punch something."

"That's sweet, Danius. I like you too."

"You can't!" He practically screamed.

"Sure I can. You're charming and not bad on the eyes either."

"No, I mean you shouldn't. And I shouldn't. There can't be anything between us. Pearl, try and understand. I've already made certain goals. My life is already mapped out. I know what I'm going to do five years from now, even ten years from now. Pearl you're beautiful and fun and I'm extremely attracted to you but you just don't…fit in my plans."

"If that ain't the story of my life." Pearl said. "I don't think I've ever truly fit in anywhere except with God."

That stumped Danius. "I'm…I just…I'm sorry. Pearl…I'm not like you. I don't just…"

"Take each day as it comes?"

"Right. I have to have a routine. I have to know what's coming next. I wasn't counting on meeting you. Now that I have, I think my whole nervous system is shutting down." He lifted his face to the sky and sighed out loud. "I…have a girlfriend, Pearl."

"Yes. You've mentioned her once or twice." Pearl nodded and looked away but didn't seem to be disappointed at all.

"You understand, don't you?" Danius asked.

Pearl didn't answer but remained fixated on whatever was behind Danius.

"Well, say something." he said.

"Glory to God." she simply said.

"What?"

"Didn't you tell the police your mother's license plate said GLR2GD?"

"Yeah, so?"

Pearl smiled and turned Danius about face. "I found your mama's car."

Trust: Not For Wimps

"Oh my…" Danius had to hold his head with both hands to keep his mind from being blown. Just ahead of him, in the beach parking lot, was his mother's Buick Regal. "Oh my gosh, Pearl!" They moved closer. "It's really here!" He said. "And it looks okay." He inspected the outside of the car, looking for dents. He found none.

"How's that for providence?" Pearl said as she approached the vehicle. "Hey, I see the keys. There in the…Oh!"

"What?"

Pearl, with wide eyes, removed her hand from her mouth and pointed at the back seat. Danius had been inspecting the headlights when he looked up at Pearl. He walked around to the rear and looked. He jumped back, bumping into Pearl. There was a man asleep in the back seat. At least they hoped he was asleep. All the windows had been rolled up, so Danius took a chance on opening the door.

Finding it unlocked, he slowly pulled it open and recoiled at the stench.

"Oh my…"

"Sweet mercy!" They exclaimed at the same time, covering their noses and mouths with their hands.

Danius heard Josiah yell, "Mom's car!" and saw Joe and the others running to meet him and Pearl but they all stumbled back into each other when they got within smelling distance.

"Whoa!" said Patrick.

"That's foul!" said Michael.

"It's putrid!" said Cary.

"It's ungodly!" said Lewis.

"Who cares?!" said Josiah holding his nose. "The car is back and I'm gonna live. Thank you, God!"

Michael patted Josiah on the back. "That's my boy! Always lookin' on the bright side."

Emily, always half a beat off, was the last to approach. "Hey! Is this the car? Ugh! What died?"

"Hopefully not the man in the back seat." Pearl answered.

They all huddled together and as one stepped closer to the car to look. No one spoke as they stared intensely at the still figure lying face down in the back seat.

"Someone really should check his pulse." Emily said, but when she looked, everyone except her had taken four steps back.

"Hey!" she exclaimed.

"You're the nurse." Pearl said through the fabric of her shirt collar.

"Yeah. It's like your hypothetical oath." said Michael.

"Hippocratic oath! And it's for doctors." Emily argued.

"Still you are a medical professional." said Danius.

"Aw, man!" She said and stomped her foot in protest. "I always have to do it. It's like the third time this week." Emily mumbled something in her native Korean as she grabbed the man's sweaty hand and checked the pulse in his wrist.

She held her breath and peered closer to check his breathing. "He's alive! And I think I'm gonna be sick." She moved far, far away from the car.

Josiah asked, "What do we do now?"

Danius pulled out his phone and was about to dial.

"What are you doing?" asked Pearl.

"Calling the police."

Pearl grabbed his hand to stop him. "No, don't call the police. They'll just put him in jail."

He gave her a strange look. "Uh…Yeah!"

"Please just wait a minute. Hear me out. I have a better idea."

How did I let her talk me into it? Danius asked himself as they waited for the Nicholases to arrive, who by some weird coincidence were only an hour away visiting relatives. Or maybe it wasn't a coincidence at all. Maybe Someone was orchestrating this whole thing.

When they showed up, they immediately went to work examining the stranger, unfazed by his odor or appearance, for they had been to the ends of the earth and back and had seen worse.

The man was in an alcohol induced state of unconsciousness; basically passed out drunk. Occasionally he would mumble or balk at being man-handled by the doctors. The only thing to do for him was to let him sleep it off.

"I still say we should have called the police." Danius told Pearl.

"Danius relax, will you? You got your car back. It stinks to high heaven but you got it back, and in one piece." Pearl said then sat down on a low wall separating the parking lot from the beach.

Danius sat next to her. "I just don't see what good any of this is going to do.

"Think about it. If Harvey goes to jail…"

"Harvey?"

"Yeah. From *Captains Courageous*. Did you ever read it?

Danius shook his head.

"Well, Harvey was this spoiled, rich kid who fell from an ocean liner and was rescued by these fishermen. And he had to live on their boat for three months, but in order to eat, he had to work. The fishermen taught him discipline, the value of hard work and how to be a man. By the time he was reunited with his parents, he was a completely different kid."

"Oh."

"And I figured, if our 'Harvey' goes to jail, they'll feed him three meals a day and give him a place to sleep. And after he's served his time, they'll turn him loose and he'll be back where he started. But if he goes with the *Iaomai* people, he'll have to dry out in the middle of the ocean. Then he'll have to earn his keep. And maybe he'll get to help somebody poorer than he is. And who knows? It could change his life. *God* could change his life; you know, make him a whole person again."

"Iaomai." said Danius. He was beginning to understand how her mind worked.

"Yeah. It says in First Samuel 2:8 *He raiseth up the poor out of the dust, and lifteth up the beggar from the dunghill, to set them among princes, and to make them inherit the throne to glory...* My brother and sister and I were once poor beggars."

Danius nodded his understanding. "You have a way of making something crazy actually make sense. It's kind of annoying."

"Thank you, and hey, if it doesn't work out, they can always push him overboard."

"Pearl!"

"With a lifeboat." She amended.

"Well, that's all we can do for now." said Dr. John when he and Amanda approached them.

"How is he?" asked Pearl.

John propped his foot on the wall and hung his stethoscope around his neck. "Well, he has a temperature. He's extremely malnourished, anemic and dehydrated"

"It's no wonder he's dehydrated. All his bodily fluids leaked out in Danius's car." said Pearl.

Danius nearly gagged at the thought.

"There's also swelling in his left forearm." said Dr. Amanda. "It may be broken but it's hard to tell when he's unresponsive like this."

We'll be able to do a full examination once we get him on the boat. said John.

"So you're really going to take him with you?" asked Danius.

John sighed. "I know it's crazy. I was telling my wife this morning that I felt like we were in for something a little out of the ordinary, but I really feel like this is the right thing to do."

"Can't wait to see the look on his face when he finds himself on the Atlantic, stone-cold sober, surrounded by a bunch of Christian missionaries." Amanda said, laughing.

"But you guys are leaving the country. What about his passport and all that?" asked Danius.

John waved him off. "Ah, that's no problem. We'll take care of it. I know a guy."

"Cool." Pearl said. "You got connections."

"Shhh." answered both doctors.

"Oh." Pearl winked and nodded.

The doctors enlisted the help of all the guys including Josiah in getting "Harvey" into the doctors' truck. After hugs all around, they said their goodbyes and were off.

If "Harvey" hadn't stolen the Buick, he wouldn't be getting the medical attention he needs. Of course, he might not have stolen the car in the first place if Danius would've taken the time to give him a couple of bucks yesterday when he asked for it. Of course, Danius wouldn't have been at that motel at all if Josiah hadn't run away. But if he hadn't run away, they never would've met the Nicholases and "Harvey" *still* wouldn't have gotten the medical help he needed. Ugh! Pearl was right. Thinking about the what-ifs only made you crazy, but Danius was amazed at how everything had come together and made sense. And now it was time to go home.

"Dude, you cannot drive back to Jacksonville with that stench." said Michael.

"It's ghastly!" said Emily

"And Jacksonville's an hour away." said Cary

"You could pass out and wreck the car…and die." said Lewis.

"Can't have that on my head, man." Michael added.

"What do you propose I do?" asked Danius

"We passed a carwash on our way here." said Patrick. "We'll take the car there and clean it up."

So the adventure wasn't quiet over yet. Danius drove the car with all the windows down to the self-service car wash with the Patiently Waiting band trailing behind him. The inside reeked of stale alcohol, vomit, body odor and all the excrement man possessed; and strangely enough, fried chicken.

"Well, Joe, it's all yours buddy." said Pearl, fanning the stench away from her face.

"What?" asked Josiah, the same question reflected on Danius's face.

"Yeah. You're sort of responsible for this little adventure, so it seems only right that you get the honor of cleaning the car."

"By myself?"

Everyone nodded in the affirmative as they stepped away from the car.

"That's not fair. It'll take me forever to get that smell out. Why are you doing this?"

"Did you think you could run away from home and not suffer the consequences?"

" Yeah." He answered matter-of-factly. "Guys, c'mon! I thought we were cool."

"Dude, we are cool. You're one of us now." said Michael.

"You're like our mascot." said Emily.

"You're the wind beneath our wings." said Lewis.

"You're also twelve years old." said Pearl. "And you did something very dangerous. And what kind of grown-ups would we be if we let you get off scot free?"

"The kind who're my friends." Josiah looked to his brother for help. "Danius, do I have to?"

If Danius wasn't impressed by Pearl and her friends before, he certainly was now. They genuinely cared about Josiah and him. He couldn't remember the last time he had real *friends*, in the truest sense of the word. "I'm afraid you do." he answered. "And if I were you, Josiah, I wouldn't complain. This is nothing compared to what Mom and Dad would've done to you."

Josiah grabbed the back of his neck and sighed in resignation. "I guess that's true."

"Good." said Pearl. "Well I'm heading over to the Starbucks across the street. Anyone want to join me?"

"Ooh! Iced Chai Latte, here I come." said Michael. "What?" he asked when he noticed Patrick looking at him in mock disgust.

"Chai Latte? That's a chick's drink."

"Yeah? And what are you gonna have, an Iced Caramel Macchiato?"

"Extra Caramel. You better man-up, boy."

Danius couldn't help but laugh at the band's antics and friendly banter as they made their way across the street, leaving Josiah by himself to wash and clean out the car. Danius was glad to know Pearl and the rest of the band only intended to leave Josiah alone with the car for an hour or so, just long enough for him to think about what he did.

"Thanks for making him do that." Danius said to Pearl. "I hadn't even thought about a punishment. I was so glad to have the car back."

"To tell you the truth, I'm tired and hot and didn't feel like washing your car."

Danius knew that wasn't entirely true, but he laughed anyway. "You're pretty good with kids. I think you'll make a good mother someday."

"Thanks. I had a lot of practice with *my* little brother."

While the band chatted over iced coffee, Danius remained quiet for the most part. His thoughts went back to the conversation with Pearl on the beach. He told himself that he had to stand by what he said. There couldn't be anything between them. He repeated that statement to himself over and over again, but when she smiled at him from across the table, he could feel his resolve slipping. He was relieved to hear Pearl announce it was now time to show a little mercy to their mascot. That meant he could busy himself with cleaning out the car and not think about anything…at least for a while.

Josiah was never happier than when his brother and their new friends came back to help him. The term "many hands make light work" was never truer. Everyone pitched in with shirts, handkerchiefs, and bandanas covering their faces. The girls took the exterior while the guys attacked the interior: shampooing and vacuuming the rugs, the floor and the seats three times each. Pearl left and returned with a can of air freshener and the biggest box of baking soda she could find. She said to keep it in the seat pockets in the back.

When they were finished, everyone changed their clothes. Danius and Josiah didn't have that luxury so they borrowed from Cary and Lewis.

And now it really was time to go.

Pearl watched Danius as he waited on his brother to change. The trip had been good for him. He looked a little less clenched than when she first met him. He reminded her so much of herself, the way she used to be. No wonder she'd taken a liking to him. She wanted to help him.

Now liking him on a personal level was a new thing for her. She had avoided romantic relationships for the most part. She went on dates occasionally but never really allowed herself to feel anything more than friendship for those men. After watching what all her mother went through with the men in her life, Pearl had vowed never to get involved with a man. She had neither the time nor desire before coming to Christ and even afterwards, all she wanted to do was serve him. But the longer she walked with the Lord, the more she began to develop into the woman he created her to be, with talents she didn't know she possessed, ambition she didn't have before and desire, once buried, now come back to life. And one of the desires of her heart stood, with arms folded, leaning against a Buick. She walked up to him and mimicked his pose. He smiled but he still looked troubled. Pearl made an attempt to lighten his mood.

"I want to thank you, Danius, for a lovely time."

"Lovely time?" He scoffed.

"Well, I had fun, robbery notwithstanding."

Danius rolled his eyes and shook his head. Pearl nudged him with her elbow.

"Hmm? Hmm?" she promted.

"Okay…there were…moments…that were not… unenjoyable."

"Your excitement overwhelms me. Seriously, tone it down a little bit."

"I'll try." He whispered as their gazes met.

It was in the unguarded moments such as this where Pearl could see glimpses of the man Danius could be if he would just let go. He loved his brother. He was courageous when he had to be. He helped out "Harvey" which proved he had a heart. And when he looked at her the way he was looking now, she could see controlled passion.

Why did she have to stand so close? She confused him whenever she got too close. Her hair smelled like some kind of tropical fruit and it looked as if she took a pair of scissors to her t-shirt. She wore it over a tank top and it hung so that it exposed her shoulder and it was driving him crazy. The form-fitting jeans weren't helping either. Alexandria didn't dress like that. Why did Pearl have to? Come to think of it, Pearl did a lot of things Alexandria didn't do and it frustrated the heck out of him.

"Pearl." He cleared his throat. "About what I said earlier…on the beach."

"My not fitting into your plans."

"Right. I didn't mean to…"

"Sound like a jerk?"

"Right. I mean I wasn't trying to…"

"Hurt my feelings?"

"Pearl!"

"Stop finishing your sentences. Okay. I've stopped."

"You're not going to make this easy, are you?"

"Well, Danius I don't think this type of thing is ever easy. But I understand. There's something going on here. We both feel it, but there's nothing we can do about it. I'm okay with it. I think."

Well I'm not. Danius thought. "Good. So…we'll just be friends then."

"Yep."

There was a brief moment of silence after that. Then Pearl giggled.

"What?" asked Danius.

"I guess if we're friends I can be honest with you. I kept your cell phone on purpose and I left it in the van on purpose." Embarrassed, Pearl smiled and shook her head.

"Why?"

"I wanted to see you again and I wanted to keep you around."

"Why?"

Pearl laughed. "Because! You made an impression on me and I like you."

Danius looked away and tried to get his mind around what Pearl had just said. Never in his life had a girl…woman said anything like that to him. What had he done to impress Pearl? He'd been rude and condescending when they first met. He had thought she was a slacker and almost told her so. What was it about him that she liked? He couldn't think of anything else to say except, "Why?"

Pearl rolled her eyes this time. "I don't know. Are you mad?"

He looked at her, smiled and shook his head. "No. I'm not mad. I'm…" He was two seconds away from taking back what he said about just being friends.

Josiah couldn't have picked a better moment to show up. Humbly, he lowered his head as he stood before Pearl and his brother. "I'm sorry I snuck into your van. But I'm kind of glad too, because I had a great time."

Pearl put an arm around his shoulders and kissed the top of his head. "Me too. And you're welcome to join us anytime…as long as you have permission."

"Okay." Josiah said right before Pearl smothered him in a hug.

"So I guess we'll see you two at the party." said Pearl.

"Well, I'll be there. I'll have to find someone to watch Joe." Danius answered.

"What?!" Josiah gave him an almost insulted look.

"You gotta bring my man, Joe." Pearl said.

"Mr. Maxwell only invited me."

"You and a guest. I'm sure he wouldn't mind. You want me to call him? I'll call him."

"No, you won't."

"Okay, but after everything that's happened do you really want to leave this kid alone?"

"Yeah." said Josiah. "I'm unpredictable."

Danius smirked at their puppy-dog expressions. "Okay. But I don't want to hear any griping about having to wear a suit."

"Deal." said Josiah

"Great!" said Pearl. "So we'll see you there." She turned to walk away.

"Wait Pearl…uh…I appreciate everything you've done. Will you tell the rest of the guys I said thank you?"

Pearl smiled and nodded then walked away.

He stared after her as she walked towards the van, his heart leaving in the same direction.

They rode in companionable silence for nearly half an hour with traces of the *Essence of Harvey* still lingering in the Buick. Danius made a mental note to shampoo and vacuum the car out one more time before he returned it to his mother.

"I think this was the best trip I've ever been on." Josiah said. "My friends are never gonna believe we stopped a robbery."

"I don't even want to think about it." Danius said. "That was very dangerous what we did."

"Yeah, but it worked."

Danius drove in silence for a moment. Josiah was right and something else he was; easy to talk to. The age difference didn't seem to matter anymore. Danius wasn't just tolerating some kid. He was hanging out with his brother and he liked it.

"Other than that," Danius said "It was…kind of fun, wasn't it?"

"I'm surprised you even noticed you were having fun. You spent the whole time staring at Pearl."

"What?"

"Dude, don't even try it. I'm twelve, not stupid. You were staring."

"I was not staring."

"You like her. I don't blame you. She's hot."

"Oh, what do you know?"

"More than you think I know. I know Pearl is a thousand times cooler than Alexandria."

"Hey, come on."

"I know you were a lot happier when you wanted to be a teacher and not whatever Alexandria and her dad want you to be."

He really did know more than Danius thought.

"And I know Pearl likes you back." Josiah said. "Just don't know why."

"I don't know why." Pearl said to Emily as they rode back to Jacksonville. "I just do. And the more time I spend with him, the more I like him."

"Wow. Of course I knew it all along, but this is kind of huge for you, isn't it? I mean, as long as I've known you, you've never acted all 'school-girlish' over some guy before."

"I've never felt 'school-girlish' before."

"So why the sad face? You like him and everybody within a five-mile radius can see he likes you. Why not go for it?"

"He has a girlfriend, remember? And I'm nobody's man-stealer. Plus, as he so aptly put it, I don't fit into his plan."

"I think your plan sucks, bro." said Josiah bluntly
"Thank you for your honesty, Josiah." Danius answered.
"You're welcome."

Two and half hours later, Danius was standing in the foyer of Mr. Maxwell's beach house inspecting his brother's suit. Though his hair did its own thing, Josiah still cleaned up pretty good for a pre-teen. Danius was a little more dapper in his single breasted, three-button, formal, black dress suit and black silk tie.

The Maxwells warmly received them and ushered them into the main room where the other guests were mingling. Josiah quickly found an ally in Mr. Maxwell's son, Freddie and they ran off to parts unknown leaving Danius to mingle on his own. That's when he saw her.

Pearl entered the main room from the patio and this time she really did take his breath away. Her crazy, mop-top had been pulled back away from her face and cascaded in curly tendrils down her back She wore a green, spaghetti-strap, satin, cocktail dress with matching heels that accentuated her gorgeous legs…she even wore actual pearls.

Danius was sure the rest of the band was decked out too as only a rock band can be, but he couldn't take his eyes off the lead singer who'd stolen his iPhone and his heart.

The main room looked more like a dance hall, Pearl thought. There was even a platform that led to the sun-deck which overlooked the beach. This would be their stage. As the band took their places, Pearl sat at the

Maxwell's Baby Grand, marveling at how beautiful it was, when she felt someone watching her. She looked up and instantly found Danius in the crowd. She felt a little self-conscious when she smiled at him, never really being one for fancy dresses, but the way he was looking at her from across the room made her feel so beautiful. Speaking of beautiful, he looked like something out of *GQ* magazine. Standing there with his hands in his pockets, he never broke eye contact with her, not even when Mr. Maxwell introduced the band.

The first half of their set was instrumental jazz. Mr. Maxwell was pleased as punch when he found Danius later on. "Todd, you enjoying yourself?" He asked, slapping Danius on the back.

"Yes, sir. Thanks again for inviting my brother."

"Oh, sure."

"I'll be sure to have him thank you personally, if I ever find him again."

"Oh, he and Freddie are watching a movie in my office. If you keep your eyes on the buffet table, you'll see one or both of them snatching food every ten minutes. It's like they're gathering food for the winter."

Danius gave a polite chuckle but try as he might, he just couldn't focus on anything not wearing a green cocktail dress right now.

"Folks, are you having a good time?" Pearl asked into the microphone. The crowd responded with a round of applause for the band. "Thank you all for coming out to celebrate the birthday of a lovely young lady, Mrs. Alicia Maxwell. Give her a hand everybody."

Danius and the crowd obeyed.

"Now, Mrs. Maxwell, we in the band were back and forth on what to get you for your birthday and we finally decided on giving you a musical history lesson. Our drummer, Michael McClure a.k.a DJ Mike is going to spin for you the hits that all the kids were rockin' the year you were born. I'm not saying what year it was, I'm just saying if I were you I'd grab my bell-bottoms, my afro pick and a pair of skates."

Michael acted as D.J. while the rest of the band took a break. Mr. Maxwell was still talking but Danius didn't hear a word as Pearl approached. Just before she got within ear shot, Mr. Maxwell slapped Danius on the back again and whispered, "I know how you feel. Kind of like being run over, isn't it?"

Danius flashed him a look but it was too late to ask what he meant.

"Pearl!" Mr. Maxwell said.

"Hello, Peaceful Ruler. How are you?" she asked.

"I couldn't be better. You all are amazing, my wife's happy and I'm racking up good husband points left and right."

Just then Mrs. Maxwell called out to her husband.

"And I see I'm needed on the dance floor. If you'll excuse me…"

"Go for the gold Frederick." Pearl said as he walked away.

Through that whole exchange with Frederick, Danius hadn't once looked away from Pearl and she'd felt it.

"Pearl," Danius said. "You look…stunning."

Wow! Stunning. She'd been called cute, pretty and even beautiful once but *stunning* was new, it was different, it made her look down at her dress to make sure there were no stains, and coming from Danius, it made her heart leap.

"Thank you." she said as she gave him a once over. "And you look…good enough to dance with."

He was never much of a dancer, but she took him by the hand and he helplessly followed. As if on cue, Michael played Stevie Wonder's version of *My Cheri Amour*. Those who were so inclined coupled up, the lights dimmed and Danius held Pearl in his arms for the very first time. His dream from the night before could not compare to this.

He held her close but not tight as they moved with the rhythm. He looked down at her, she looked up at him and somewhere in the background, Stevie sang to his *Cheri Amour* but it was as if they danced to a different song that only they could hear. And it played in both their hearts.

Danius leaned his forehead against hers, wrapped both arms around her waist and brought her closer. He couldn't hear anything now, just his heart beating and aching for Pearl in a way he never had and never would for Alexandria.

His hands were warm on her back but Pearl still trembled in Danius's arms. Did he have any idea how broad his shoulders were or how his arms could make a woman feel safe or how the scent of his after-shave could make a girl dizzy…in a good way? For years there had been chains around her heart, keeping her from loving and being loved by a man. But in time she'd learned how to give those chains to God and the longer she abided in him the more his truth had made her free and was still *making* her free.

It was in this moment, on the dance floor, that she felt the very last chain snap. In that moment she could say with assurance, she was falling for the ultra-serious, schedule keeping Danius Todd. The thought warmed her all over. *"Oh God, what do I do?"*

"Let him go." The words were spoken into her mind but couldn't have been clearer if Jesus had shouted them in her ears.

"Let him go? What do you mean?"

"He's not ready for a relationship. You have to let him go."

"Please God. I love him." she argued internally. She held Danius tighter and he responded in like manner.

"I love him more." said the Spirit of God. *"There's a lot I have for him to do and you would only be a distraction."*

"Oh, God please don't do this to me now. I love him."

"Then let *him seek me, for his sake. Will you trust me?"*

Danius wasn't aware of the struggle Pearl was having, he was too busy free-falling; his heart spiraling out of control. There was no use in fighting it anymore, so he just let it happen. Who knew where or in what condition he would end up? Pearl's arms were wrapped around him and he felt safe and she felt so good in his arms he could weep but when she became tense, he knew something was wrong. He pulled back to look her in the eyes. They were filled with unshed tears. She looked vulnerable and so very desirable. He lightly placed a hand on her cheek as Stevie Wonder crooned the exact words of Danius's heart. *"… How I wish that you were mine."*

"Oh, Pearl." The words came out deep and raspy. He didn't know where he got the boldness but he fully intended to kiss her in that moment. And he would have too, if she hadn't pulled back and walked away.

The song had ended and in its place something with a faster tempo played. More people gathered to dance but Danius stood there in the midst of them watching Pearl retreat to the sun-deck.

What was he doing? What was happening? This thing between Pearl and him was in no way part of the plan. Alexandria calling at precisely that moment further confirmed that fact. He didn't answer, only stared at Alexandria's name all lit up, like a beacon to guide him away from the raging storm within him. This was his future: Alexandria, law school, her father's firm, a house in the San Marco area with three kids who all attend private school.

All at once he felt pulled in two different directions: by what Pearl represented and by what Alexandria represented. The obligation he felt towards Alexandria was strong but whatever it was he felt for Pearl was even stronger and that's why he found himself stepping out onto the sun-deck.

The moon was high in the sky and its light made the sand glow. The breeze off the water wrapped itself around Pearl and brought with it the smell of the ocean. Pearl leaned against the railing and inhaled deeply.

Why was she struggling? She'd been walking with the Lord long enough to know his voice. So why was she debating whether it was his voice or her own? Because for the first time since coming to Christ, she wanted something-someone-with such a passion that it took her breath away. But God was asking her to give it up. Give him up. And she didn't want to.

"Will you trust me?" He asked again.

Pearl closed her eyes and whispered yes into the breeze. She did feel a small measure of peace and imagined God smiling.

She heard the click of the glass door behind her and didn't even have to turn around to know who it was.

The Breaking Point

There she stood with her back to him. Pearl wouldn't turn to meet Danius, so he approached her carefully. Not knowing what to do with his hands, he almost placed them on her shoulders but decided at the last moment to place them on the railing as she had. About a minute passed before either spoke.

"Are you okay?" Danius asked.

"I just needed some air." she said. "It was getting kind of warm."

Another minute of silence passed.

"There's an elephant on the sun-deck." said Pearl.

Danius smiled and nodded. "Do you want to talk about it?"

"I don't know what to say."

"Pearl McClure is speechless? I'm shocked."

"Danius Todd made a joke? *I'm* shocked."

Danius couldn't help but notice how close his hand was to hers. He stared fixated. He longed to touch her again. "I almost kissed you."

"I wanted you to."

"Then why did you walk away?" He took a chance and grabbed her hand but she pulled away. Rejection hit him in the chest.

Should she tell him about hearing the voice of the Lord? She wasn't afraid to. It was just, at this point, she didn't think Danius would understand. "I seem to recall your saying there can't be anything between you and me."

"Pearl, don't."

"Don't mention that? Okay I won't. How 'bout this; you have a girlfriend."

He sighed in frustration.

"You don't like that one either? Okay then. How 'bout; I don't fit into your plan."

"My plan sucks!" Danius smacked the railing with his hand. "There, I said it. Are you happy now? My plan sucks! Josiah said it earlier today and I couldn't agree with him more, all right? I don't want to be an instruction writer. I don't want Alexandria or her father's prestigious law firm. I don't want to be a lawyer…I don't want to be a *lawyer*! Oh my…" His eyes widened at that revelation. It made him so dizzy, he had to brace himself with both hands on the railing.

"You don't?"

"No! I don't want to be a lawyer. I don't want to live in San Marco. It's way too expensive. I mean, it's nice if you can afford it, but I can't. And what is so wrong with public school? There are a lot of good ones out there."

"I liked my school." Pearl said timidly, not sure where he was going with his rant.

"So did I!" He put a hand on his chest and took a few deep breaths.

"Okay…so then…what do you want to do?

"I don't know. Everything is a jumbled mess. It's like there was a tornado in my brain and all that's left is the wreckage. I can only make heads or tails out two things and that is: You ruined my life and I really, really…like you."

She turned away from him and faced the ocean, desperately trying to remember the promise she had just made to God. "You have the worst timing of anyone I've ever known." she said.

He placed his hands on her shoulders and this time she didn't pull away. Leaning his forehead against the back of hers, he let his hands travel up and down her arms and reveled in the exotic fragrance that clung to her.

Danius was so close she could feel his breath on her neck. She shivered when he whispered in her ear. "You feel so good. Pearl, I don't know what to do. I can't even think right now. All I know is that I want to be with you."

God help me. She prayed and turned around to face Danius. She fiddled, nervously, with his tie. "You can't. We can't."

"Why?" He asked as he grabbed her arms.

She tried to pull out of his grasp. "Danius, please."

"No. Tell me why." He said, tightening his hold, but mindful not to hurt her.

"You and God have a lot to sort out and I would only get in the way."

"What? No." He shook his head.

"Danius, listen to me. You're in a very good position. You have no idea what to do about anything right now. And that's not a bad thing, because maybe now you'll ask for help. God has a better plan for you than anything you could ever imagine…tailor-made just for you. You need to find out what it is and to do that, you have to seek Him."

Pearl looked inside and saw the band reassembling. "Intermission is almost over." She moved to go back inside when Danius once again placed a hand on her arm.

"What about…" He gestured with his hand in a back and forth motion indicating the connection between the two of them. "Will I…see you again?" he asked.

"If you ever get a hankerin' for folk-music and coffee." she said with that trade-mark wit he had come to love. "I'm gonna go inside before I cry my eyes out right in front of you."

"We can't have that." Danius said, his voice choked with emotion.

"It was fun, wasn't it?" she said, not waiting for an answer. She took her hurting heart back inside and rejoined the band for the second half of their set.

Danius was left standing alone with the sound of waves breaking behind him. If he had to describe how he was feeling at that moment, "numb" would be the most appropriate word. "Numb" and maybe "weightless." As if he'd been shot up with anesthetic then shot into space. There he was, just floating with no direction, until he asked, "What now?" And slowly but surely began to sense the gravitational pull toward something.

Change of Plans

The party was a smashing success. Mr. and Mrs. Maxwell were so please with the band, especially during the second half of their set, that they insisted on paying them extra. Indeed, Mr. Maxwell gushed well into the next day. Of course, he couldn't have known that the lead singer was in pain at the time. She'd sung so passionately and was such a ham on stage. He also couldn't have known his instruction writer was suffering as well. Or could he?

To make up for missing his Friday appointment with Mr. Maxwell, Danius decided to skip church and get right to work but Mr. Maxwell had other plans.

First, Danius and Josiah would join the Maxwells for an early-morning worship service. Then they'd all have brunch at the house, shoot the breeze for an hour or so and then get to work.

Danius really was in no mood for church but agreed anyway. Per Mr. Maxwell's instructions, he and Josiah dressed casually and joined the Maxwells on the beach for an open-air, sunrise service.

They sat on the sand among surfers, bikers passing through on their way to Daytona, a guy with a metal detector and joggers who decided to stop and listen to a bare-foot man in shorts and a t-shirt with the sleeves cut off talk about Jesus.

It was unconventional and Danius had never seen anything like it. Mr. Maxwell later explained that the speaker was an ordained minister who felt called to take the Gospel of Jesus outside the four walls of the church. Danius didn't know whether it was the sea air, the sunrise or the sermon or a combination of all three that lifted his spirit but sure enough, whereas he was numb before, he now felt pain and that was a step in the right direction. The barefoot preacher talked about becoming a whole person through Christ and Danius soaked it up like a sponge

"The dictionary defines the word 'whole' as: sound; healthy; restored; healed." said the preacher. "In Greek the word is *Iaomai*: To heal or to make whole. That's what Christ wants to do for us: To heal us and make us whole. I mean, we walk around here like we have it all together but because of sin all we really are, is broken. But that's why Jesus died on the cross; for the sins of the world and so that we could be healed and restored with a sound mind, and reconciled to God which in effect makes us whole human beings, full of faith and purpose

'This may be hard to believe but I use to walk around in Armani suits, making boat-loads of money. Nothing wrong with that, right? But what good did all that money do me when my wife wanted to leave me and my kids didn't want anything to do with me?

'I was so miserable, I put a gun to my head. I had just about convinced myself to pull the trigger when my little boy walked in on me. All he said to me was, 'Don't Daddy! Jesus wouldn't like it!' I'm telling you the truth, man. It broke me. And I spent the rest of the night curled up on the bathroom floor crying like a baby. All night long, all I could say was "Help me, Jesus. Help me, Jesus"

The preacher opened up his Bible. "In the Bible, in the book of Jeremiah chapter 33 verse 3 it says, *'Call to me and I will answer you, and will tell you great and hidden things you have not known.'*

'That night was a new beginning for me. I told Jesus all the things I did wrong and He forgave me. In time He helped me make amends with my family. He restored my marriage, He restored me...made me whole. Now I work as a means to provide for my family, but I *live* for Christ. That's my purpose; to serve Him and tell other people about Him."

That's when Danius realized how broken he was and that this whole weekend had been about this moment. He thought Pearl had been the reason his world turned upside down, but it was God the whole time.

"Are you all right?" asked Mr. Maxwell. "Why don't you take a walk? I'll watch out for your brother."

Up until then, Danius hadn't even noticed the tears streaming down his face. He left the group and walked a ways by himself. When he was sure he was alone, he let the tears fall liberally. Then he spoke from his heart. "Jesus…I feel so lost. I don't know where I went wrong. I don't know anything anymore." He knelt in the sand facing the ocean and the sunrise.

"That's not true. I know I shut you out of my life and tried to live according to my own plans and I've been miserable and empty ever since. But God, please forgive me. I want to be yours again. I want your plan, whatever it is."

Danius cried in earnest now. "Please forgive me." he whispered. "Make me whole."

He spent the rest of the morning getting reacquainted with his Creator. Funny, but Danius always remembered that day as the day he woke up from a very long sleep

The days that followed proved to be a challenge. It was a challenge adjusting to a new way of life; no longer being the captain of his soul. He'd finished his job for Mr. Maxwell and was on to another assignment but now he felt unsettled; like he didn't belong there. He'd asked God for guidance and one day, out of the blue, Josiah asked him what the word, *commiserate* meant and while trying to explain it, the desire to teach - a desire Danius had long ago suppressed - resurrected with such force, it shook him.

It was a challenge explaining all of this to Alexandria, but Danius sat her down one day and told her everything - well almost everything - about his adventure, about Josiah running away, the *Patiently Waiting* band and their music, the auto theft, the robbery, the Nicholases, "Harvey" and how it all sort of came together to make him see how much he needed God.

And despite the fact Alexandria professed to be a Christian and was an avid church-goer, she just could not or would not see God's hand in the situation.

"What does any of this have to do with your not going to law school?" she asked.

"I don't want to be a lawyer." he said. "As long as I can remember I have always loved science and history and literature. I want to teach. I believe that's what God wants me to do."

"To work at a thankless, grossly underpaid job? Listen to me. Look around you." Alexandria gave a sweeping arch of her house. "All of this is going to be mine someday and by extension, possibly yours. And what's so wrong about going into law? It's a noble profession. The right field of law could afford you a lifestyle other people only dream about. Now don't you want to think it over?"

He wasn't mad at her, he wasn't even annoyed. As a matter of fact, he felt quite at peace, but that still didn't stop him from putting a little edge in his voice when he looked her in the eyes and said, "I-don't-want-to-be-a-lawyer."

Alexandria looked stunned but only for a moment. She crossed one long leg over the other and lifted one perfect eyebrow and said, "Then you don't want me."

Unfazed, Danius stood and planted a kiss on her cheek. "At least we agree on something. Goodbye Alexandria."

Danius walked out feeling a hundred and twelve pounds lighter.

Then there was the challenge of telling his parents the truth about the car, which Josiah was flatly against. The challenge wasn't in *telling* them the truth it was in getting them to *believe* it. In the end they laughed at the far-fetched story and Gloria just waved it off saying, "I'm just glad you returned the car in one piece. But please, no more eating soul-food in my car. That smell is hard to get out of upholstery…smelled like collard greens and fried chicken in there." To which Danius and Josiah both said, "yes ma'am," and left it at that.

The greatest challenge for Danius though was trying to forget Pearl, a woman he'd only known for four days but knowing her had changed his life. He missed her so much it hurt, especially at night when there was nothing left to do but think.

He came across a scripture one day in Proverbs that said, *"Trust in the Lord with all your heart and lean not to your own understanding, but in all your ways acknowledge him and he will direct your paths."* Putting this into practice was not easy. Oh, trusting God to guide him on the right career path was all right but in matters of the heart it was rather difficult, because he was drawn to Pearl and had been from the very moment she walked up to his table.

His attraction to her had turned into physical desire and-dare he say-love. But as Pearl had said, he and God had some things to sort out. Danius knew that but it didn't make it any easier. Nevertheless he let God in on the situation, how he felt, and trusted God to direct his path.

For the next year and a half it didn't seem like Danius's path was being directed anywhere near Pearl. While other areas of his life seemed to improve by leaps and bounds, his love life was null and void. He'd been set up on a few blind dates by his parents and friends from church and those girls were attractive but that's all they were. None of them seemed to radiate light and warmth from the inside out. None of them frustrated Danius to the point of distraction. None of them had that strange mix of child-like simplicity and age-old wisdom from experience. None of them could tug on his heart because Pearl already had it.

Danius knew the past year and a half had been more about establishing his relationship with God than finding a soul mate. It had been about becoming the man he was created to be, but how was he expected to continue on without Pearl if she was never far from his thoughts?

Seeing flyers posted, advertising her café and its goings-on didn't help at all. One of them even had a picture of her and the band on it, stating that *Patiently Waiting* would be performing "Friday Night at 7pm." He saw them posted all over town. The only place he didn't see them was at the beach. He had made a habit of going to the beach every Saturday morning for a jog during sunrise. It was a great way to relieve the stress of the week and to talk to God. Of course, God was probably getting tired of hearing him talk about Pearl. Even when Danius purposely changed the subject, his prayer would always end with something about Pearl. To which God would always reply, "*Just trust me.*"

Running into Mr. Maxwell on one of those Saturdays only compounded his frustrations. Mr. Maxwell greeted Danius warmly, suggested he come back to the beach house in the near future and to bring his brother, asked him what was new and then proceeded to tell him all about recently attending some sort of party given for computer programmers; strictly black-tie, live music stuff. When, who do you suppose happened to be there?

"Pearl?" asked Danius.

"Yeah, the whole band was there. It turns out that one of the guests at my wife's birthday party liked the band so much that he hired them to play for the programmer's party that he was facilitating. Oh, they were great! I wished you could've been there. Pearl was in rare form that night. And it was so good to see her again."

"Oh, really? That sounds...I really wish I could've seen her--them, the whole band." Danius asked, his throat about as dry as the sand they were walking on.

"Yeah. That was about two months ago. I haven't seen her since. How's she doing?"

"Uh...I don't know. We...I...haven't seen her since the night of your wife's party."

Danius must have had one sour looking face because Mr. Maxwell looked at him with pity when he said, "Oh, no. It didn't work out between you two? Gosh, you made such a nice couple."

"Well, Mr. Maxwell, we were never...I mean, she and I weren't...we're just friends." That last word tasted like acid in his mouth.

"Oh, yeah. I remember you saying something like that. But Todd, I watched the two of you that night and I have to tell you, you have about as much luck convincing yourself as you have of convincing me that you and Pearl are just friends. And I'm not convinced."

Danius only nodded at that.

"How are you feeling?" asked Mr. Maxwell.

"Like I've been run over."

Mr. Maxwell laughed at that, remembering what he said to Danius the night of the party. "Yeah, I know the feeling. Alicia Ann McGuire ran me over twenty-two years ago and I'm still trying to get up. Why don't you do something about it?"

"I can't. It has to do with me and God and the fact that she would only be a distraction. Look, I love God. I want to seek him. I want to serve him. But how can I serve him effectively if I can't stop loving some girl?"

"You and I both know Pearl isn't just *some* girl. And I don't think God has called you to be a eunuch, Todd. He's called you away for a season to be alone with him and get to know him and seek his will for your life and to learn how to trust him. I believe in due time, God will release you to go look for the one who'll *help* you live out the will of God not *distract* you from it. And if I know anything, something tells me you've already found her. You just have to wait, son."

Danius let out the most pitiful sigh as he lowered his head. All Mr. Maxwell could do was laugh.

"I know. Waiting sucks, right?"

"Good Lord, it sucks so bad!" Danius laughed in spite of himself. Being told he would just have to wait for Pearl was not what he wanted to hear, but it turned out to be just what he needed to hear. That being said, it still didn't improve his mood, but it did give him a little peace while he waited just a little longer.

On one particular day--the day after his last disastrous blind date--Danius was leaving the college where he was taking courses to earn his teaching degree. Feeling border-line depressed, he prayed out of frustration, "God I don't know how much more I can take. I keep comparing these other women to Pearl and that's not fair. I'm acknowledging you like you said. So will you show me what to do about my feelings for Pearl? If I'm not supposed to be with her, then please take these feelings away."

Let it never be said that God doesn't have a sense of humor. For at that moment, as Danius was walking up to the bus-stop, a black Chevy Vandura Camper with red pin stripes passed him. He stood there with his mouth open for what seemed like an eternity. He didn't even notice his bus approaching until it stopped.

"Oh Lord, what do I do?" he asked out loud.

"You *could* get on the bus." answered the driver.

"Or you could go get her." said the Lord. And he didn't have to say it twice. Danius took off after the van on foot.

The thought occurred to Danius that a man running down State Street in a suit and tie with nobody chasing him probably looked ridiculous, but he didn't care. All he wanted to do was see Pearl. He wondered if he still had a chance, did she still feel the same way or had she moved on. If she had, what would he do?

No! He wasn't going to talk himself out of this. Besides, he heard the voice of the Lord plain as day telling him to, "Go get her." And that's what he planned to do. As for what he'd say to her when he got there, he'd just have to wing it.

As he bobbed and weaved through pedestrians, skirted oncoming traffic, and stupidly crossed I95 Expressway during the evening rush hour, the words of a song his mother was singing the other day played over and over in his mind.

> *I'm gonna love you*
> *Like nobody's loved you*
> *Come rain or come shine*
> *High as a mountain*
> *Deep as a river*
> *Come rain or come shine*

When he'd asked her about it, she let him listen to it on her Judy Garland's greatest hits album. The song had a frenetic beat that rivaled his foot falls and the pacing of his own heart at that moment.

As he neared the street that would take him to The Q café, he made a promise to himself and to God that if he indeed had a chance with Pearl, he would do everything in his power to live up to the lyrics of that song.

It was closing time at the café. Pearl had finished the ritual of balancing the register and cleaning the dining area and now she sat down with her band mates who were involved in a serious discussion.

"No!" said Lewis.

"Why not?" asked Michael.

"It just isn't. That's ridiculous."

"It's a perfectly valid question. Why shouldn't the opposite of raw sewage be cooked sewage?"

A round of "eews! and ughs!" echoed in the otherwise empty café.

"All in favor of changing the subject *please* say aye." Pearl said.

"Aye!" said everyone but Michael.

Nevertheless, he moved on. "Okay. You wanna change the subject? We'll change the subject. Why do you keep blowin' off my man, Andre?" he asked Pearl.

"Ugh! I'd rather talk about cooked sewage."

"Oh no. Answer the question."

"Which Andre are you talking about, 'bank' Andre or the Andre that makes me itch?"

"The Andre that's into you. I asked you and you said you'd consider going out with him."

"Yes I said I'd *consider* it and I did; and only because I thought you meant the one at the bank not the one with the side effects."

"Don't exaggerate."

"I'm not exaggerating. I'm allergic to your friends."

The band laughed and joked like that for an hour. Though she laughed right along with them, Pearl mentally chastised herself for once again finding fault in a guy who was interested in her. She'd been doing that for the past year and a half, but how could she help it? None of them sparked her interest. None of them had eyes so warm they could melt butter. None of them had ever looked at her with something more than just physical attraction. None of them could tug on heart because Danius already had it.

Not a day went by that she didn't think of him at least once. Every time she had to read the instructions for something she wondered if those instructions were written by him. Things like, "Shake well before opening." Or "Apply a small amount of our rich cream onto your hands and massage until absorbed into your skin." Or even the more intricate, "How to use stopwatch: In 'Normal Time Display Mode.' Press 'M' button twice." Even when she purposely refused to read the instructions for setting up her new Blu Ray disc player she still thought of Danius.

She thought of him even when she went on the one and only date she'd agreed to since meeting Danius. The guy was nice enough but she knew it had been a mistake. Pearl felt bad especially since he was the cousin of one of her baristas and friends, Sheena.

The day after, as she and Sheena were restocking the shelves with more flavored syrups, they went over what went wrong.

"Everything went wrong. It wasn't his fault though. It was all me. I just wasn't all there last night." Pearl said.

"Well, where were you?" Sheena asked while reaching to place the syrups on the top shelf.

"Slow dancing at a fancy party on the beach in my spaghetti-strapped cocktail dress, with a man who smelled like Old Spice."

"Ooh, did he look like the Old Spice guy?"

"Way better!"

"Hmm. It must be love, 'cause no one looks better than the Old Spice guy. 'He's on a horse.'"

Pearl shook her head and handed Sheena another bottle for the top shelf.

"Wait a second." said Sheena. "Is this that same uptight, iPhone guy?"

"Yep."

"Oh…well, I guess you could do worse."

"Thank you."

"But I don't get it. Why are you breaking my sweet cousin's heart when you could be dating this other guy?"

Pearl searched for a way to word it without going into a whole narrative. "The timing is all wrong, I guess. He's on a journey and right now I would just be in his way."

"I still don't get it."

Pearl looked up at the six-foot-two Sheena and decided to have a little fun with her. "I wouldn't expect you to understand. I mean your brain is at a higher altitude than the rest of us. The air is thinner up there."

"Oh, here you go with the tall jokes. It's too early in the morning for all that."

"You're right. Let's just stock the shelves, Avatar."

"Avatar? That's funny. Here I am trying to help you out with your little love life and you're cracking jokes."

"You're right. I'm sorry. You know I wouldn't mess with you if I didn't care. "Cause honestly, Sheena, I really look up to you."

Sheena blushed and smiled but the flattery was short lived when she realized Pearl had made another joke. "Shut up!" she said good-naturedly.

Pearl laughed out loud. "Gosh! You make it so easy." Joking around with Sheena was a good diversion, but thoughts of Danius were never too far away. And it wasn't long before he once again took center stage in her mind.

It would be so easy to just "happen to be in the neighborhood" and stop by his apartment. Or call him just to say "hello." But every time she felt her resolve weakening, God would whisper the same words she heard the night of the party, *"Will you trust me?"*

"Oh God." she would say. "I'm trying to trust in you. Maybe if I knew one way or the other what your plan was concerning Danius and me, I wouldn't be so miserable. Lord if it's meant to be then show me how to wait with patience. If it's not, then help me get over him once and for all. I don't want to pine after someone I can't have for the rest of my life."

The whole thing was crazy anyway. She'd only known him for four days and hadn't seen him in eighteen months. But what an amazing four days it was, though. She had set out to teach Danius how to have some fun, and had ended up having the best time of her life. But what was the use of hanging on to something that just wasn't going to happen? Still, even knowing this, she wished Danius would just walk through that café door right now.

Never let it be said that God doesn't have impeccable timing. For at that very moment, there stood a man bent over banging on the glass door. Pearl moved towards the door. When he stood a bit straighter, she recognized him. He was panting and pouring with sweat but he never looked better. Their eyes met and they stood there staring at each other until he pointed at the lock on the door.

Pearl unlocked the door and Danius fairly stumbled in.

"As I live and breathe!" said Emily.

"It's the dude!" said Michael.

"Whatup, iPhone?" asked Patrick.

Danius, bent over with his hands on his knees, still trying to catch his breath, did his best to greet them. "Guys…I was…at…college…saw your van…ran here."

"You ran all the way here from the college? Why?" Pearl asked.

"I…love…" Danius would have finished that sentence if everything hadn't gone black.

He opened his eyes and found himself on a cold, hard-wood floor with his feet elevated and six faces staring down at him.

"What happened?" he asked.

"Well, you had an interruption of normal blood circulation to the brain, causing an abrupt yet brief loss of consciousness." said Nurse Emily.

"Huh?"

"You passed out." said Cary.

"You fainted." said Lewis.

"It was lights out for you." said Patrick.

"Somewhere over the rainbow." said Michael.

"It's good to see you all." said Danius.

Pearl knelt down beside him and caressed his cheek with the backs of her fingers. "How do you feel now?"

He couldn't speak. Her simple touch sent his blood racing. There was a good chance he might pass out again. He leaned into her touch. They weren't speaking but the others heard them loud and clear.

"Uh…let's give Danius some air." said Patrick as he shepherded the others toward the kitchen. "Pearl can stay here and help him…you know, with his air."

"Hey Pearl?" said Michael. "You mind if we get some frozen yogurt?"

There was no answer.

"Free yogurt?"

Still no answer.

"We-are-not-paying-for-the-yogurt."

The others rushed Michael into the kitchen before Pearl got wise.

Now they were alone. Neither one made a move to get off the floor. Pearl finally broke the silence. "90 degrees in the shade and you ran all the way here. Why didn't you take the bus?" she said in that soft, sweet way he remembered.

There was this chair that belonged to Danius's grandfather. It was a huge leather recliner. Danius loved that chair. Something about it just gave him a sense of peace; the way it engulfed him. Being in Pearl's presence had the same effect.

"I didn't think it all the way through. I just wanted to get here." The color was returning to his face as he spoke.

"Why the rush?"

"I've wished I could see you every day for the last 18 months. So when He said go, I went."

"He, who?"

"A really good friend. I knew Him as a child but we lost touch until I met Him again on a beach last year. You know Him too, better than I do, but I'm getting there."

Pearl smiled and lit up the whole room. She knew who he was talking about. She looked deep into his eyes. That little lost boy look that was there when they met was gone. In its place was the look of a man at peace.

"What'd you want to see me about?" she asked as if she didn't know.

"Well, originally it was to tell you I'm desperately in love with you and I want to spend the rest of my life with you. But now I'm thinking that's probably too much to deal with all at once. So how about I just ask you out to dinner? That is…if you're not already seeing someone."

"You're asking me out on a date?"

"Every Friday night for the next sixty or so years."

A single tear slipped down her cheek and Danius reached up to wipe it away.

She shuddered at his touch.

"Oh, Pearl." he whispered. "I missed you so much."

"What about your plans?" she asked.

Danius sat up and faced Pearl. "Plans change. You know that Friend I was telling you about? Well He seems to have a different plan, and honestly, I think it's better than anything I could ever come up with."

That was all she needed to hear. Impulsively, she kissed him. The contact sent shock waves through them both. Then grabbing the back of her neck, Danius pulled her closer and deepened the kiss.

"So does this mean you will go out with me? He asked, holding her at arm's length.

"I don't know. My Fridays are pretty tight. But I think I can squeeze you in."

"Well, whatever you can do." He closed the distance between them and kissed her with restrained passion, knowing this was only the beginning.

Loving Pearl was going to be a life-long adventure.

"Aw, poor Andre." Michael said as he and the band stood in the doorway with their frozen yogurt, watching Pearl and Danius fall in love.

"Don't worry. There's plenty of fish in the sea for Andre to chafe." said Patrick.

Epilogue

"Hey, slow your roll, Mister! We ain't married yet." said Pearl; the back of her neck tingling where Danius kissed her.

"I know and it's killing me." He sighed into her shoulder.

She finished packing his lunch and turned in his arms to face him. "I know, baby, me too. But summer will be here before we know it and then we'll get our 'Holy Matrimony' on."

Danius laughed. "I'm looking forward to it."

Pearl reached up, wrapped her arms around his neck and kissed his waiting lips. Oh how she loved this time of day: morning time. Danius would stop by the café before it opened and Pearl would fix him breakfast and pack a lunch for him, then they would end up in each other's arms. She hoped to continue this little tradition they started after they married.

Danius was feeling particularly nervous about today so he clung to the two things that gave him the most comfort: his faith and his Pearl. She was a wonderful gift in his life. She encouraged him the whole time he was in school, was patient with him while he continued to navigate his way out of being an uptight, control freak to trusting in God and giving Him control, and she had a way of knowing what he was thinking.

"Don't be nervous." she whispered against his lips.

"How about a kiss for luck?" He stole another sweet kiss from her.

"You don't need luck. You're gonna be great. I'm talking, *Lean on Me* great; *Stand and Deliver* great; I'm talking about *To Sir, with Love* great."

"Wow! Sidney Poitier, really? I'll take it."

"Hey Danius." said Josiah poking his head through the kitchen doors.

"That's Mr. Todd to you, young man." said Pearl.

"Excuse me. Mr. Todd, if you're done makin' out with your girlfriend, can we please go to school? We're gonna be late."

"Since when are you anxious to get to school?" Pearl asked.

"Since he discovered that ninth grade boys get to lean against the wall before school and check out the ninth grade girl parade." Danius joked.

"Right." squealed Josiah, his voice in the process of changing. "And if I want a good spot, I have to get there early."

Pearl grabbed the two lunches she made and handed them to Danius and Josiah. "In that case let's not keep the man waiting."

Josiah looked in his bag and smiled. "Free food. I am going to love having you for a sister." Turning to Danius--he was almost tall enough to look him directly in the eyes now--he said, "And you. If you break her heart, I will break your neck."

"Is that any way to talk to your teacher?" Danius asked.

"Substitute teacher. For six weeks. And only from eleven to twelve."

"Okay. Don't give him a hard time." said Pearl.

"He ain't had a hard time yet. It's his first day and he's the *substitute*. He's gonna get eaten alive."

There was silence between the three of them. Danius let those words sink in.

Then Pearl broke the silence. "Well, if there's anything left of him after school, make sure you bring it here because the Nicholases are in town and we're having dinner with them. Oh, and they're bringing Henri Richard with them. I love that name. It's French; *Awn-ree, Ree-shard.*

"Who?" asked Danius.

"You know. *Harvey*!"

"Oh!" Danius and Josiah both said.

"Yeah. They're stopping over on their way to Haiti where Henri is from. His family still lives there. Wait 'til you see him. You won't recognize him."

"Will they be here for my competition this weekend?" asked Josiah.

"We can ask them."

"All right. Well, Joe." said Danius making his way to the door. "Let's go. You can escort me to my execution."

Pearl gave him a reassuring pat on the back. "Hey now, I told you you're going to be great. You'll teach them how to dissect things and blow stuff up. They'll love you. You know, I have a feeling you're going to be *that* teacher; you know the one that kids grow up and remember for the rest of their lives like Mr. Chips? Have you seen that movie? They'll be 40 years old still talking about the teacher who taught them that molecules are a metaphor for life. By the way, did I mention I love this tie on you? Green is your color and it's so soothing to the eye."

When she paused long enough to take a breath, Danius took that moment to kiss her one more time. "Bye, honey." he said.

"Goodbye Mr. Chips. Have a great day."

"I still say he ain't got nothin' on the Old Spice guy." Sheena said from across the room.

"Who asked you, Stretch?"

Danius left the café with Josiah, ready to face this new chapter in his life. He had no idea what to expect. He would just have to trust God would see him through. But he supposed that was God's plan all along.

The End